Fire GIRL

MATT RALPHS

MACMILLAN CHILDREN'S BOOKS

First published 2015 by Macmillan Children's Books
an imprint of Pan Macmillan
20 New Wharf Road, London N1 9RR
Associated companies throughout the world
www.panmacmillan.com

ISBN 978-1-4472-8355-3

Text copyright © Matt Ralphs 2015
Illustrations copyright © Fred van Deelen 2015

The right of Matt Ralphs and Fred van Deelen to be identified as the author
and illustrator of this work has been asserted by them in accordance
with the Copyright, Designs and Patents Act 1988.

To Mum and Dad,
for everything

CONTENTS

Pull the rope to ring the bell,
Chase the devil back down to hell.
Set the trap with loop and wire,
Drive the stake in the vengeful fire.
Catch her soul in a silver sieve,
And suffer not the witch to live.

Traditional English nursery rhyme

PROLOGUE

Wychwood Forest, England, 1656
Twelve years after the end of the Witch War

Mary Applegate awoke with a lump of fear lodged in her throat.

There's someone in my room.

She lay still as a corpse, sensing for the presence – the *thing* – she felt sure was watching her, but all she heard was the whisper of trees and the distant screech of an owl. There was nothing to explain the sense of unease plucking at her nerves. Nothing except a faint coppery smell, like warm blood.

Her elbows cracked as she sat up in bed. 'Foolish old woman,' she muttered to herself. 'It's just a dream.'

Cold air prickled her skin. Grumbling to herself, she wrapped a blanket around her shoulders, struggled out of bed and limped down the stairs. Her old bones ached with every careful step.

The front door creaked on its hinges, letting in the smell of rain and wet leaves. Wondering whether she'd forgotten to lock up before going to bed, Mary pulled it closed and slid the bolt home.

The wood-and-plaster walls felt rough under her fingers as she hobbled around the kitchen to the fireplace. Flames crackled when she stirred the embers and threw on a few logs.

'Oh, Gander,' she sighed, holding her cold hands over the flames. 'Were you but here, you silly old thing.'

Since the death of her goose-familiar, Mary's dark world had become darker still. She missed Gander's voice and company so much. Sometimes she fancied that she heard his webbed feet slapping on the floorboards behind her, but it was only ever an echo from her fading memory.

Shaking her head, she hung a saucepan of spiced mead over the hearth and settled down to wait for it to warm up. Its sweet smell soon filled the kitchen, lulling her into a restless sleep.

A furious hammering at the door woke Mary. She jerked her head towards the noise, her heart fluttering like a trapped moth. No one visited her any more, especially not at this time of night.

'Who's there?' she called, creeping towards the door. 'What do you want?'

There was no reply.

Taking a deep breath, she drew back the bolt and opened a crack in the door. The air was brittle with frost; birds fidgeted in the trees, their wings rustling like parchment.

'Cold as the grave tonight.' A man's voice, soft and

2

deep as quicksand. 'May I come in?'

He pushed open the door and strode past Mary without waiting for a reply.

'Who are you?' she cried, turning on the spot to follow his movements.

'Just a traveller seeking shelter from the cold. Did I startle you?' He was close enough for Mary to feel his breath on her cheek.

'It takes more than a late-night visitor to startle me,' she muttered, masking her fear with a frown.

'Is that so?' The stranger sounded amused. A chair creaked as he sat down at the table. 'My, what a lovely fire.'

Mary felt a stab of annoyance. *Coming here uninvited, and in the middle of the night no less*, she thought. *The cheek!*

'Is that mead I smell?' the man asked. 'I'd appreciate a cup to warm me.'

It was customary in Wychwood to help those in need, no matter how inconvenient the time. Mary gritted her teeth. 'Very well,' she said.

'I don't suppose you get many visitors, living so deep in the forest.'

'None at this hour, certainly.' Mary carefully placed the saucepan on the table, gathered two cups from a shelf and sat down opposite the man. 'So, are you lost?'

'Lost?' The man chuckled. 'No. I know exactly where I'm going. Shall I pour?' The aroma of mead drifted between them as he filled the cups.

3

The silence extended until Mary snapped, 'So where *are* you going?'

'Rivenpike.'

'That dreadful place? You won't find anything there except shadows and ghosts.'

'Nevertheless, to Rivenpike I am bound.' The man shifted in his chair. 'Although I took a small detour to visit you . . . *Mary Applegate.*'

'How do you know my name?' she spluttered, nearly choking on her drink.

'Oh, I know all about you. I know why you live out here alone. I know who blinded you all those years ago, and why they did it. I know exactly who and *what* you are.'

Fear tightened around Mary's throat. 'Are you . . . a Witch Hunter?'

'On the contrary.' The man chuckled again. 'You really don't recognize my voice? Well, it has been some years, I suppose.'

Mary searched her memories . . . his voice *did* sound familiar. 'No,' she breathed. 'It can't be. *Nicolas?*'

'Yes, I am Nicolas Murrell, our former King's Chief Minister of Magic and Witchcraft.'

'But . . .' Mary shook her head in confusion. 'I thought you'd been captured and taken to the Tower?'

'So I was, Mary, so I was. And there I remained in Lord Cromwell's . . . *care* . . . for far longer than I'd like to remember. But I escaped, and now the hunt is on to find me again.' A note of satisfaction entered his voice. 'You are

4

playing hostess to the most wanted man in England.'

Mary's legs wobbled as she stood up. 'I want you to l-leave,' she stuttered. 'Now.'

'But I've only just got here. Please, sit down.' He rapped his knuckles on the table. 'Sit.'

Frightened, overwhelmed, Mary obeyed.

'So tell me, Mary, why have you hidden yourself away in Wychwood?'

'I fled after we lost the Witch War,' she replied, fiddling nervously with the silver bracelet around her wrist. 'The forest is the only place I'm safe now.'

'Not for much longer. The Witch Hunters are widening their nets. Cromwell wants you disposed of, once and for all. There are no safe places for witches, or those who sympathize with them, any more.'

Mary picked up her cup with trembling fingers. 'I've heard that the Coven is fighting back in the North.'

'They are, but their campaign is faltering.'

'I've prayed for their success,' Mary said.

'Yet you've stopped short of joining their ranks?'

Mary shrank from the contempt in his voice. 'I'd be no use to them. Besides, I've seen enough war to last a lifetime. I want no part of it.'

'So what *do* you want?' Murrell asked.

Mary seized her courage, leaned forward and said, 'To be left alone.'

'I'm afraid that's just not possible.' Murrell's words oozed into her ears like syrup. 'I want *you* to help *me*.'

5

'What can a blind old hedge-witch do to help someone like you?'

Murrell laid his cold hand over hers. Mary flinched when she realized that his thumb was nothing more than a blunt stump.

'I want information,' he said, squeezing her fingers.

'Why should I tell you anything?' Mary whispered, wishing she could control the tremor in her voice.

'Because I'm going to give you something in exchange.'

The chair scraped as Murrell stood up and strode around the table to stand behind her. Mary froze as he grabbed her head with both hands and pressed his fingertips against her eyelids. He muttered under his breath and a bright white pain stabbed into her skull.

'Stop,' Mary choked, trying to push his hands away. 'What are you doing?'

'I am giving you a *gift*,' Murrell said, letting her go. 'Open your eyes.'

Mary blinked. Colours swirled in front of her eyes as the blindness that had veiled her sight for decades began to lift. Shapes swam into focus: the stained dining table, the glowing hearth, and shelves lined with jars, pots and copper pans.

'What have you *done*?' Mary cried, wishing she had the courage to turn around and face him. 'You're not a Wielder – you shouldn't be able to cast magic. What dark witchcraft is this?'

Murrell's shadow loomed over her. 'I think you know.'

'Demonic magic?' Mary gasped. 'Oh no . . . You were always reckless, Nicolas, but to consort with demons . . .'

'Needs must in these dark days.'

'You cannot trust a demon – you know as well as I do that they'll betray you in a heartbeat. Tell me, what did you give up in order to gain this magic?'

'I am prepared to make any sacrifice to save our people,' Murrell said. 'Unlike you.'

Mary breathed deeply, fighting to slow her heartbeat. She looked at the winding blue veins and the shape of finger bones visible through her tissue-thin skin. 'I look so old,' she said.

'Time has less mercy than I do,' Murrell said, resting his hands on her shoulders. 'And to prove it I'm going to give you a chance to atone.'

'Atone for what?'

'For abandoning your people and giving up the fight against the Witch Hunters,' he replied. 'Now, *quid pro quo*, Mary. I have only one question to ask you. If you answer truthfully, I will leave you alone. But if you lie—'

'Spare me your threats,' Mary said, sounding braver than she felt. 'Just say it.'

Murrell bent down so his mouth nearly touched her ear. '*Where is she?*'

Mary squeezed her eyes shut, knowing who Murrell was asking about. *Not that*, she thought. *I can't tell you that.*

Murrell leaned more heavily on her shoulders. 'Well?' he said.

Mary tried to sound nonplussed. 'Where's who?'

'Now, Mary, you know better than to play me for a fool. I know you know who I'm looking for.'

'I have no idea *who* or *what* you're talking about,' Mary spat. 'You are not welcome here. Get out of my home.'

'I was hoping it wouldn't come to this,' Murrell sighed. 'But I think it's time to introduce you to your second house guest. Rawhead, come out and greet our hostess.'

The door to the cupboard under the stairs creaked open, unleashing the same coppery scent of blood she had sensed in her bedroom.

'Come here, Rawhead,' Murrell said. 'Come and sit at the table.'

A shadow moved inside the cupboard, and then a bone-coloured head, smooth and featureless except for two gaping nostrils, emerged into the flickering firelight of the kitchen. A skinless beast of flesh and sinew loped towards the table, its black-clawed feet and hands scratching the floorboards.

A demon, Mary thought. *It was watching me while I slept. It's been here all this time!*

Murrell picked up his cup. 'Delicious mead. Most refreshing.'

Mary pointed a shaking finger at the demon. 'By the power of the moon goddess, I command thee to leave this place.'

The demon yawned, exposing even ranks of wicked

teeth. Its serpentine tongue quivered across the table, tasting the air.

'Your feeble magic won't have any effect on Rawhead,' Murrell said. 'You should count yourself lucky, witch. Few people get the chance see such a powerful demon; fewer still survive to speak of it.'

Mary shrank back as the beast leaned towards her, hot breath jetting from its nostrils. 'Summoning demons breaks the laws of magic,' she said.

'I've chosen to overlook them.'

'You have no *right*. What if the binding spell fails? What if you were to die and this . . . *abomination* was allowed to roam free with no master to control it?'

'We are at *war*, Mary. We need weapons with which to fight. Now – to business. Where . . . *is* . . . she?'

Mary steeled herself. 'I don't know who you're talking about.'

'Liar.'

Mary stared at the table, lips pursed together.

'Rawhead's hungry,' Murrell said. 'Perhaps he'll start with your feet?'

The old witch closed her eyes as the demon champed its drooling jaws.

'I'll give you one last chance, Mary Applegate,' Murrell continued. 'Where can I find Hecate Hooper?'

I
WITCH'S GLADE

Witches are wise, cunning folk, clever with herbs
and healing. The most skilled – known as Wielders –
harness magic to cast spells and charms.
Notes on Witchcraft and Demonology by Dr Neil Fallon

The Glade, Wychwood Forest, three days later . . .

Hazel Hooper strolled along the orchard path, whistling quietly and enjoying the sun on her back. Beams of light slanted through the trees, turning the floating cherry blossom into flakes of gold. It was a perfect summer's day in the Glade, the only home she had ever known.

She plucked an apple from her basket and took a huge bite, letting the juice dribble down her chin. *Just right for a pie*, she thought.

She froze, mid-munch, as something large and orange burst out on to the path in front of her. It was Ginger Tom, her mother's bad-tempered cat-familiar, with whom Hazel was in a perpetual state of war. Something small and furry dangled in his jaws.

'Tom!' Hazel shouted. 'What have you got there? Oh, you horrible creature – it's a poor little dormouse.'

Bursting with rage, she hurled her apple as hard as she

could. It flew over Tom's head and exploded against a nearby tree, showering him with sticky pulp.

'Pick on something your own size,' she said as he dropped the mouse and disappeared yowling into the under-growth.

Dropping her basket, Hazel picked up the limp dormouse as gently as she could and enfolded his shaking body in her hands. She closed her eyes, searching for a spark of magic and muttered a healing spell painstakingly memorized from her mother's books.

'*Magia-mus-sanaret,*' she whispered. As usual, nothing happened.

'Hold on, little mouse,' she said, pushing her disappointment aside. 'Ma will set you right.' She scampered out of the orchard into a well-tended vegetable garden. At the end of the path was a cottage with a sagging thatch roof and flowers rambling around the door. Hazel dashed breathlessly into the kitchen. 'Ma, look what I—'

A foul smell stopped her dead. Barely visible through a veil of greasy steam stood Hazel's mother, Hecate. She was staring into a simmering cauldron with one hand on her hip and the other stroking her chin.

'What *is* that smell?' Hazel gasped, fighting the urge to choke. 'More Boggart repellent?'

'Mmm, it needs something to liven it up, doesn't it,' Hecate murmured. 'Be a love and pass me some briar-wort, would you?'

'In a minute, Ma. First, look at what Tom did.' Hazel

11

held out the dormouse. 'All your good-for-nothing familiar likes to do is torment animals smaller than him. He's such a bully.'

'He may be my familiar, but that doesn't mean he doesn't still have his animal instincts,' Hecate said. She frowned at the mouse. 'His leg's broken and he's had a shock, but I think I can help him.'

Hazel watched transfixed as her mother muttered an incantation – '*Magia-mus-sanaret*' – touched her lips to the mouse's nose and exhaled a silver mist. A few moments later, the dormouse opened his eyes and sat up, brushing his whiskers with a newly healed front paw.

'I tried that spell, but it didn't work,' Hazel said, carefully setting the mouse on the table-top.

'I'm sure you did your best,' Hecate said, putting a lid on the bubbling cauldron. 'Perhaps we should open the windows . . .'

'But shouldn't my magic have appeared by now? I'm old enough, aren't I?'

'Well, yes. But . . . we've talked about this, Hazel. The chances of you becoming a Wielder are very slim. We're a rare breed.'

'But I *want* to be like you,' Hazel said. 'To have my own familiar, and heal things and . . .'

'I know you do.' Hecate sighed. 'But believe me, it's much safer if you remain an ordinary, un-magical girl.' She patted down Hazel's tangled red hair. 'You could run a comb through this every so often. And I see you've been climbing trees in your best dress again. Look, the stitching's coming undone.'

I wish you wouldn't treat me as if I was a little girl, Hazel thought, her temper flaring.

'Mary's coming to see us soon,' Hecate added, interrupting Hazel's thoughts. 'She's bringing that book on herb-lore I was telling you about.'

Hazel rolled her eyes. 'Great,' she muttered.

'It's got a very informative section on toadstools that I think you should read,' Hecate said with one eyebrow raised.

'I said I was sorry about picking the wrong sort,' Hazel bristled. 'I didn't mean to poison us with that pie.'

'I know,' Hecate smiled. 'I'm only teasing.'

Hazel watched the dormouse waddle towards the fruit bowl and tried to calm her angry mood. It was too nice a day to spoil with an argument. 'Is it true Mary's familiar died last month?'

'It was Gander's time to pass on,' Hecate said.

'So she's all alone?'

'Well, she has us.'

'But she *lives* alone. She must be so lonely.' The dormouse was struggling to climb into the fruit bowl so Hazel gave his portly bottom a lift and he tumbled inside.

'Mary's a tough old bird and used to her own company.'

'But she's blind and getting old, Ma. I think it's sad – no one should be alone *all* the time.'

Hecate sat down at the table and took Hazel's hand. 'I'm

13

sure you have a suggestion to remedy this, as usual?'

'Well . . . why don't I go and stay with her – keep her company? Just for a day or two? When she comes to visit I could go back with her and—'

'You know you can't leave the Glade,' Hecate said.

'But it'd just be for a couple of days . . .'

'No, Hazel. No. We can't go beyond the Border Hedge. We've talked about this.'

'We haven't, not properly.' Hazel pulled her hand away. 'You've told me we can't leave, but never explained *why*.'

'You're too young to—'

'I'm nearly twelve!'

Hecate jabbed her finger on to the table. '*Exactly*.'

'I just want to know why you're keeping me here like a *prisoner*.'

'But . . . this is our home.' Hecate's face fell. 'I thought you loved the Glade?'

'I *do*,' Hazel said. 'But I've been stuck here my whole life. I want to see the rest of England. I want to meet other people apart from you and Mary. Why don't you understand that?' She yanked at her red curls in frustration. 'I mean, are you really going to keep me here *forever*?'

Hecate looked down at her clasped hands. 'You don't know what it's like out there.'

'Then tell me. I just want the truth. I deserve to know.'

'My little girl's growing up.' Hecate smiled sadly and ran her hand down Hazel's cheek.

'That's what I'm trying to tell you, Ma.'

'Perhaps it is time you knew.' Hecate plucked the startled dormouse from the fruit bowl. 'I'm going to let this fellow go, then take a dip in the pool to clear my head. We'll talk when I get back.'

2
A DEMON AT THE DOOR

Demons are unholy creatures in endless forms most foul.
Glimpses of the Demon Underworld
by Grand Magus David Ellefson

Hazel watched through the doorway as Hecate skirted the pool and put the dormouse down by a willow tree. *What is it about England that frightens Ma so much?* she wondered. The prospect of finally knowing was as exciting as it was terrifying.

Dandelion seeds sailed on the breeze and hunting swallows swooped and dived over the glittering water. Hecate, her hair burnished in the sun, waded waist deep into the water. The scent of honeysuckle drifted into the kitchen, carrying with it a faint coppery undertone that Hazel couldn't quite identify.

As the smell got stronger, it awoke a feeling of dread in the pit of her stomach. She stood up, banging her leg on the table and upsetting the fruit bowl. Apples rolled and fell to the floor with heavy thumps. Hazel reached the door in time to see something under the water break away from the bank and glide up behind her mother.

A creature with a domed, eyeless, bone-white head

slipped through the surface of the pool. Higher it rose – tense, poised, its clawed fingers folded like a praying mantis ready to strike.

At last Hazel's throat loosened and she cried out, but before Hecate even had a chance to look around, the creature pounced, grabbing her throat and waist and lifting her clear out of the pool. She thrashed and struggled as it dragged her towards the far bank, her legs kicking up silver arcs of water.

For an electrifying moment, Hecate locked eyes with her daughter. 'Run, Hazel – *run*!'

But Hazel didn't move. Rage such as she had never felt before exploded in her, boiling away her fear. 'Leave my mother alone,' she screamed as the world turned red.

The air around her crackled as her heart pumped so much magic through her veins she thought it would crack her skull in two. With a shriek, Hazel threw out her arms and unleashed a boiling wave of fire across the garden towards the pool.

The creature twisted on the spot, shielding Hecate as the firestorm broke across its back and staying silent even as its flesh burned and peeled away.

Hazel's ferocious magic spluttered and died. She crumpled to the ground like a dropped puppet, raising her head just in time to see the demon disappear through the trees, cradling her mother as gently as a new-born baby.

3
BRAMLEY MOUSE

Hazel awoke, half drowned and gasping. Frozen from skin to soul she lay on the ground, one arm outstretched as if grasping for a lifeline. Thunderclouds growled, hurling rain, their bloated innards charged with lightning.

Ma, she thought. *Where is she?*

Her throat felt raw. Racked with thirst, she slurped from the puddle she lay in. The gritty water gave her just enough strength to wobble to her feet. Memories crashed down over her: the eyeless demon and her mother's terrified face – but most vivid of all was the fire-magic pouring from her fingers. She lifted her hands, certain that they would be covered in blisters and blackened skin, but they were unscarred.

The grass and reeds around the pool were burned brown, and the air still carried the taint of brimstone and magic. *Her* magic. In the distance lay the forest, smeared across the horizon like charcoal on wet parchment.

What was that . . . thing? Why did it take Ma? Hazel

wondered, scanning the land for any signs of them. *Is she even still alive?*

Tugging strands of sodden hair from her face, she ran back into the cottage and started throwing open drawers and cupboards. She filled a shoulder bag with bread, cheese, dried meat, a pocket knife, a small pouch of coins and a few spare clothes. Then she changed into a dry dress, her hobnailed ankle boots, shrugged on a red hooded cloak, hurried to the door – and froze.

The land outside the Glade was unknown to Hazel, and she had *longed* to see it. But now, when desperate need was forcing her to leave, she couldn't even find the courage to step out of her own cottage door. She searched her heart for some hope, but all she found was doubt and fear.

'Come on, Hazel,' she whispered, clenching her fists. 'You *can* do this.'

'You're not going out in that weather, are you?' said a high-pitched voice.

Hazel spun around. 'Who's there?'

'I am.' The voice sounded annoyed.

'Er, who . . . ? Where are you?'

'You're not very observant, are you? Look down. No, over *here.*'

Hazel gaped. Sitting on the upturned fruit bowl, with a look of twitchy indignation on his face, was the dormouse.

'Close your mouth,' he snapped. 'It makes you look like an imbecile.'

Hazel found her voice. 'You can . . . talk?'

19

'Evidently.'

She bent down, scooped him up and held him in the palm of her hand. His fur was warm and soft. 'I don't believe it.'

The dormouse stood on his hind legs and shook a claw at her. 'How dare you pick me up without asking?'

'You can actually *talk*.' Hazel continued to goggle at him. 'But *how*?'

'With my mouth, of course. See how it moves in time with my words? Although, I grant you, before now I could only talk to other animals.' He glanced around anxiously. 'By the way, where's that horrible lump of a cat?'

The air crackled with magic and Hazel nearly dropped the dormouse as flames erupted from his fur. Heat shimmered and his tail glowed like a hot poker, although all Hazel felt was a warm tickle. After a few seconds the flames died away.

'What was *that*?' she cried.

'I don't know,' the dormouse wailed. 'It's been happening ever since I got caught in your little fireworks display down by the pool. I'm all *magical*, and I don't like it. You need to be more careful who you aim at.'

'*I* did that to you?'

'Yes.' The dormouse shook his head in disgust. 'There I was, minding my own business, when you hit me with your stinky magic. None of my friends are going to speak to me any more, and I don't blame them.' He glared at Hazel, whiskers splayed. 'I blame *you*.'

She plonked herself down in a chair and stared helplessly at him. 'I'm sorry. I didn't know I could cast any kind of magic till today. It just sort of bubbled up. At least it didn't hurt you.'

The dormouse sniffed. 'Well, try not to let it happen again.'

After an awkward pause Hazel said, 'Do you have a name?'

'Of course I have a name. All animals have names. Mine's Bramley, after my favourite food.' He stared pointedly at the spilt apples.

Hazel put him down on the table, picked one up and cut off a slice with her knife.

'Ta,' Bramley said.

'I'm Hazel. Hazel Hooper.'

'Well, Hazel Hazel Hooper, seeing as you saved me from that cat earlier – I suppose I can forgive you.'

Hazel stared through the door towards the forest. 'I must go,' she said, almost to herself.

'Nonsense. Look at that downpour. It'll wash you away.'

'I *have* to go.'

'Well, don't blame me if you catch a chill,' Bramley said, rubbing his paws along his whiskers to clean off drops of apple juice.

'I've got to find my mother. But what can I do against that . . . *thing?*'

Bramley plopped on to Hazel's lap and looked up at her. 'More than you think – you're not just an ordinary girl.'

'I'm not?' Hazel frowned.

'You cast magic, didn't you? So that means you're a . . . ?'

'A Wielder.' Saying the words sent a thrill down her spine. 'I'm a Fire Witch.'

'Correct! Now, I'm going to make a nest in your hair,' he said, clambering up her dress and poking his head into her dark red curls. 'I assume you have no objections?'

'Are you coming with me then?'

'Well, obviously.'

Hazel shook her head. 'But why?'

'I can see that I'm going to be the brains in this partnership,' Bramley said. 'Go on, *think*.'

'Oh, I see! You're my familiar.'

'Lightning strikes at last,' Bramley said, burrowing further into her hair.

'But how . . . ?'

'Well, I heard stories when I was a pup about animals who were struck by magic and started talking to witches. I always hoped it would never happen to *me*.' He reappeared above Hazel's other shoulder. 'Oh, this one appears to be much the same as the other one,' he said with a note of disappointment.

'I see,' Hazel said. She supposed that the company of an irritable rodent was better than no company at all. 'I suppose we'd better make the best of things, hadn't we? And yes, you can make a nest in my hair as long as you promise not to poo in it.'

'What do you think I am – a common rat?' Bramley

22

pressed his warm fur against her skin. 'Now let's get going, if we must.'

'I think . . . I think the thing that took Ma was a *demon*,' Hazel whispered.

'A demon, eh?' Bramley squeaked. 'Are they all as ugly as that one?'

'I don't know, but ugly or not we're going to track it down.' Hazel picked up her bag and stepped into the rain.

'I had a nasty feeling you were going to say that,' Bramley said.

4
THE BORDER HEDGE

*Some witches are able to command the
natural world for honest purposes, such as
healing animals, or creating bountiful harvests.*
A Study of Benevolent Magic by Titus White

With Bramley clinging to her ear, Hazel followed the demon's trampled trail through the trees, unsure if the tang of blood hanging in the air was real or imaginary. All she knew was that if she allowed herself a single backwards glance at the cottage, her courage would shatter and she'd hide under her bed and never come out.

I've got to think about Ma, she thought. *I must be strong for her.*

She emerged from the shadows of the orchard into a meadow, feeling small as she stared up at the roiling black clouds. Drizzle hung indecisively in the air.

Scolding herself for wasting time, she waded into the rain-battered reedgrass and down the slope towards the Glade's border. Ankle-deep mud sucked at her boots and soon she was red-faced and panting.

'Will we be gone long?' Bramley asked from somewhere deep in her hair.

'What?'

'From the Glade, I mean. When will we be coming back?'

'How should I know?' Hazel snapped, realizing she had no plan, no idea what was going to happen to them both.

'All right, don't tie a knot in your tail.' He wriggled out of his nest and settled down on her shoulder. 'Now, where are we going?'

'I don't know that either,' Hazel replied. 'I'm just following the trail. Why don't you *think* before you ask stupid questions?'

'Have you always been so bad tempered?'

Hazel took a deep breath and started to count to ten.

'*Well?*' Bramley persisted.

'Only since I met you.' An angry bloom of fire rippled over her skin before vanishing with a hiss.

'You need to learn to control your magic,' Bramley said, his own fur sparking in return. 'I can see travelling with you is going to be a very *trying* experience.'

Hazel's clothes were soaked through by the time she emerged from the meadow on to a puddle-strewn path.

'What,' said Bramley in a squeaky voice, 'is *that*?'

They looked up at an immense hedge, stretching out of sight in both directions, as tall and solid as a Bronze Age earthwork. Glossy leaves overlapped like dragon scales, and brambles with inch-long thorns threaded through the foliage like parasitic worms.

'The Border Hedge,' Hazel whispered. 'It surrounds the Glade. There're no gaps or gates in it – believe me, I've looked hard enough.'

'You never tried to cut your way through?'

Hazel shuddered. 'That would be very dangerous.'

'Why?' Bramley said, sniffing the air suspiciously. 'It's only a plant.'

'Not just any plant. Ma enchanted it to keep things out of the Glade.'

'Oh. What sort of things?'

'She never told me. Bad things, I suppose.' Hazel rubbed a leaf between her thumb and finger; it felt warm and waxy. 'Sometimes I think I can hear it breathing, almost like it's alive. Can you feel it?'

'What nonsense!' Bramley squeaked, diving behind Hazel's ear and trembling.

'Look,' Hazel said, spotting a buckled mass of branches near the ground. 'This is where the demon must have come through.'

She lowered her hood, shook out her red curls, then crouched down to peer through the hole in the hedge. As her eyes adjusted she saw an endless labyrinth of vicious-looking brambles fading to darkness. She rocked back on her heels. 'But how did it get past the enchantment? Only Ma and Mary know the spells to grant safe passage.'

'Please tell me there's another way through,' Bramley said. 'Dormice are allergic to the dark. It makes us come out in bumps.'

'I thought dormice were nocturnal?' murmured Hazel, frowning into the dark.

'Well, not this one!'

Hazel gently plucked the tiny mouse from behind her ear and held him up to her face. 'I don't have any choice, Bramley. I'm going in and that's the end of it. If you want to stay behind . . . well, this is your last chance.'

Bramley huffed but didn't say anything.

'Right then.' She tucked him securely into a small pocket at the top of her cloak and took a final look back at the Glade.

Her heart broke for the second time that day; the landscape she loved was lost behind a drab curtain of steel-grey rain, and her mother's magic that had fed the plants and flowers was being washed away into the mire. The end of the Glade had come, wrapped in a cloak of cloud and thunder.

I'll be back, she thought, and like a swimmer preparing for a dive, took a deep breath and plunged into the Border Hedge.

The air turned humid as she forced her way through the outer skin of leaves into the Hedge's innards. She groped forward, straining her eyes against the gloom, keeping one arm above her head to keep trailing brambles out of her face.

Bramley's muffled voice emerged from the pocket. 'In the unlikely event of us ever making it out of this hedge, what can we expect to find on the other side?'

'England.'

'What's an "England"?'

'It's not an "an", it's an "a". A country.'

'Oh,' Bramley said. 'And how big is *a* England?'

Hazel frowned as she forced her way through a tangled net of foliage. 'I don't know. Ouch! Damn these brambles.'

'And you've never been there?'

'No,' she said, wiping away a trickle of blood from the back of her hand. 'Ma created the Glade before I was born.'

'Why?'

'I don't know,' Hazel said. 'She never told me, even though I asked her loads of times.' A fiery anger welled up within her as she thought of all the secrets her mother had kept. *Clearly she didn't trust me at all.*

The further Hazel went, the more cramped the tunnel became, forcing her to stoop even lower. Stinging sweat ran into her eyes. The treacle-thick air was getting harder to breathe. Something creaked close by; it sounded like a noose being twisted. A coil of fear tightened in her stomach. Vines pulsed, drawing closer together, shutting out the last glimmers of light.

'Bramley?'

'Yes?'

'Did those vines move because I disturbed them, or . . . ?'

'*Or* . . . ?'

'Or did they move on their own accord?' Hazel glanced over her shoulder. 'I can't see the way back,' she said. 'The passage has closed up.'

'Then stop bleating and *move*.'

'It's swallowing us,' she moaned, turning on the spot.

28

'The Hedge knows we're here. It isn't going to let us out. We're trapped—'

With the sound of a whip crack, a vine lashed out and sliced her cheek. Hazel fell backwards with a cry.

'Hazel,' Bramley squeaked, tugging her ear. 'For pity's sake, run!'

Fear gave Hazel the strength to shove her way through the criss-crossed web of vines, but she knew she would not get far. The Hedge had them in its grip and wasn't going to let them go.

We're going to die in here, she thought, her breath coming in panicked gasps.

Brambles tangled in her hair and snaked around her throat. She squealed as a root emerged from the ground and wrapped itself around her ankle, sending her sprawling face first to the ground. She lay in the suffocating darkness as the constricting weave of brambles closed in, gulping and squirming like an eel on a dried-up riverbed. The bramble around her neck drew tight, biting into her skin.

'I can't . . . *breathe* . . .'

Bramley scuttled out from her hair and pinched the tip of her nose with his claws. 'Listen to me,' he said. 'Use your fire-magic – it's our only chance.'

'I can't,' Hazel wheezed. 'I don't know how.'

'Think back, how did you feel when you first let the fire out?'

Hazel closed her eyes, remembering . . . 'Anger. I felt so *angry*.'

29

'Then feel it again.'

'I . . . I'm too afraid.'

Bramley's fur ignited and the brambles flinched away from the heat. 'So you're giving up?' he said. '*Pathetic*. Look at you – call yourself a Wielder?' Hazel yelped as he pinched her nose again. 'You're nothing but a silly little girl. Your mother's better off without you.'

'Stop it!'

'Not until you *fight*!'

Hazel screamed with rage as magic erupted from her skin, lighting up the darkness and burning the vines away. Eyes wide and shining, Bramley clambered back into her hair.

'That's it, witch-child, *burn it all down*.'

Hazel struggled to her feet, breathing hard. Wreathed in flames and smoke, she took a step forward, then another. Foliage melted away as she advanced, whipping back into the shadows to escape her fury. Snake-like roots retreated underground, leaves quivered and burned to ash.

'Come on, Hazel,' Bramley cried. 'We're nearly there. Don't give up now.'

Hazel staggered on, feeling her anger wane, her flames turning red like dying embers in a hearth, until, with a final effort she forced her head and shoulders through the scorched leaves and out into the open. Gasping for air, she dragged her legs clear of the Hedge and flopped on to the ground. As her eyes rolled up in their sockets, the final flames around her guttered and went out.

5
BEYOND THE HEDGE

*After the Witch War, England's witches fled to the
wild parts of the land. It is best to avoid such places,
unless travelling with adequate protection.*
The Prudent Traveller by Gerhardt Ohler

'Wake up, Hazel, *wake up*. There's something coming.'
Hazel forced her eyes to open. Wet, cold and covered in scratches, it took her a moment to realize she was in a forest, lying half submerged in a pile of damp leaves by the towering Border Hedge.

A creaking roof of interlocking branches arched high overhead. Shafts of grey light cut through the leaves to the forest floor, and lumps of fungi like melted wax clung to tree trunks, glowing with an eerie green light. The air was heavy with mist, but at least the rain had stopped.

'How long was I asleep?' Hazel mumbled.

'Hours,' Bramley said, fidgeting by her ear. 'I thought you'd never wake up. Now hide, for goodness sake.'

Hazel winced as she stood up. 'Oh, my poor head . . . it's pounding. And my mouth tastes of ashes. I didn't know using magic would be so painful.' She wrapped her cloak tighter around her shoulders. 'I'm outside the Glade. I can hardly believe it.'

'Stop being so dozy and *listen* to me,' Bramley yelled, giving her ear a nip. 'Something's coming. Can't you smell it?'

Hazel sniffed; under the smell of earth and leaves drifted the unmistakable tang of blood. 'The demon – it's come back.' Her skin crawled.

'That's what I've been trying to tell you,' Bramley said. 'Now *hide* before it finds you.'

Hazel limped across the clearing, searching for somewhere to conceal herself.

'In there, in *there*,' Bramley squeaked – tugging her ear until she spotted the hollow trunk of an ancient oak tree.

She ducked inside and out of sight. Insects crawled through the flaky wood as Hazel put her eye to an empty knothole and peered out. Leaves drifted down and settled on the ground. The forest held its breath. Silence fell.

Hazel stifled a gasp as something moved through the mist and stopped by the Border Hedge. The smell of blood caught in her throat, making her gag.

It's here . . . she thought, pressing a hand against her mouth.

Through the knothole she saw a bulbous, eyeless head, raised high and waving left and right as though sniffing the air. A pinkish ridge of bone ran from its shoulders and down its spine to a gristly spike of tail. Hazel watched with horrified fascination as it loped on all fours towards the Hedge, exposed muscles bunching and stretching.

'Rawhead, wait.' It was a man's voice – something Hazel had never heard before.

The demon stopped and turned its blank face towards the speaker. A tall figure swept into the clearing, face hidden by a dark hood. A cloak of black feathers, shining like an oil slick, brushed the ground as he passed the tree.

He must be the demon's handler, Hazel thought.

As the man knelt down next to the demon and draped a pale arm over its neck, Hazel saw that his right thumb was missing.

'I need the girl alive and unharmed, just like her mother,' said the man, stroking the demon's jaw. 'And bring Hecate's familiar too, if you can find it. The ginger cat.' He moved his mouth to within inches of the demon's face. '*Try* to refrain from eating it.'

With a thrust of its legs, the demon was gone, swallowed up by the Hedge. Bramley shuddered, his trembling whiskers tickling Hazel's ear.

The man stood up; for a moment his gaze fell on the oak tree. Hazel looked into eyes so black they looked like empty sockets. Then he turned and seeped back through the trees like smoke in the dark.

Hazel slumped to her knees, her heart racing.

'Come on,' Bramley whispered. 'Time, I think, to go.'

6
WYCHWOOD

*'The full might of the Order of Witch Hunters is set
to fall like a hammer on the witches of England.'*
Lord Protector Oliver Cromwell

Hazel ran through the forest, leaping over roots, ducking
under branches and bursting through drifts of leaves.
She might have run forever if she hadn't tripped and fallen
flat on her face. Bramley rolled off her shoulder, squeaking
with each bounce.

'Have you always been so clumsy?' he spluttered.

'Only when I'm running away from a demon,' Hazel said,
wiping mud from her face. She looked around to ensure
they were not being pursued. The mist had evaporated and
above, through the swaying branches, was a bright blue sky.
Her spirits lifted at the sight.

'That man,' she said. 'Who do you think he was?'

'I've been shaken about so badly I can hardly think
straight,' Bramley huffed.

'If he's keeping Ma alive he must need her for something.
And he came back for me and Tom.'

'The demon-thing can eat that horrible cat for all I care.'

'Bramley!' scolded Hazel. 'I *know* you don't mean that.'

34

She scratched her nose thoughtfully. 'What possible use could *I* be to anyone?'

'I'm racking my brains,' Bramley muttered.

'Wait a second!' Hazel leaped to her feet. 'If we follow them – they might lead us to Ma. We have to go back.'

'Are you totally mad?' Bramley said. 'How long do you think it'll take that demon to catch you? I wouldn't give a rotten acorn for your chances.'

'Well, what other choice is there?' The curls of her red hair started to smoulder.

'There are *always* other choices. You're just not giving yourself a chance to think of them.'

'If I wait I might lose her forever—'

'Listen,' Bramley said, his whiskers twitching in agitation. 'When that demon discovers you've left the Glade it's going to come looking for you, and you'll be no good to your mother if you're captured too. We need to get as far away as possible and *then* think of a plan. I for one have no intention of becoming demon food – if it's all the same to you.'

Hazel's shoulders slumped. 'I suppose you're right,' she said in a shaky voice.

'I usually am. Now pick me up. You've got walking to do. And pick some berries as you go. I'm *starving*.'

Wet leaves squelched under Hazel's feet as she wandered further into the forest. After years of tramping over the same hills and meadows in the Glade, it felt strange to be somewhere new, a place not hemmed in by boundaries.

Bramley had been very quiet for the last hour or so. Hazel peered into her pocket and found him curled up into a ball. She poked him with a finger.

'Wassat? Wha? What?' mumbled Bramley.

'Are you sleeping?'

'No,' sniffed the mouse. 'Well, maybe. We've been walking for *hours*. I'm tired.'

'*I'm* the one who's been walking for hours,' said Hazel. 'And I've come up with a plan, if you can stay awake for long enough to listen to it?'

'Go on then,' Bramley said.

'We're going to find Blind Mary,' said Hazel.

'Who's Blind Mary?'

'A good friend of Ma's. She's a Wielder too, very old and clever. Going a bit doolally, to be honest, but I know we can trust her.'

'She sounds splendid,' Bramley said. 'Where does she live?'

'In the forest.'

'This forest?'

'Yes,' Hazel said, turning on the spot and peering through the trackless trees.

'I don't suppose you know where *exactly*?'

'Er, well . . . no.'

'Why does that not surprise me?' Bramley shook his head.

Hazel tapped him on the nose. 'That's enough, mouse. Now,' she continued as Bramley sulked, 'all we need to do

36

is find someone who knows where she lives. There must be a farm or town nearby. The first thing to do is get out of this forest.'

'But which way do we go?' Bramley shimmied up Hazel's cloak and gripped on to her ear.

Hazel grinned and pointed up. 'We climb the tallest tree we can find and take a look.'

'Wonderful. Just wonderful,' groaned Bramley.

'That one looks easy to climb,' she said, pointing to a copper-leaf beech tree.

'I think the most sensible thing would be for me to stay down here.'

'Scared?' Hazel asked, hauling herself on to the lowest branch.

'Certainly not! I was . . . er . . . just thinking that if I was on the ground, I could catch you if you fell.'

'Now why didn't I think of that?' Hazel laughed. 'But don't worry, I won't fall. I used to go climbing in the Glade all the time. I'm like a squirrel.'

Bramley gripped her ear even tighter. 'Fine,' he said. 'But for goodness sake, stop talking and concentrate.'

The sunlight brightened as Hazel wormed her way through the branches until, panting for breath, she poked her head through a gap in the leaves. A breeze brushed her face, carrying with it the distant rattle of a woodpecker. Wychwood shimmered in the sun, rolling and swaying like an ocean. Leaves hissed like waves on shingle, branches creaked like masts.

37

'Oh, Bramley, it's beautiful!'

'I'll take your word for it,' he replied. 'Just tell me what you see.'

'Treetops as far as the horizon, green and copper and red. The sun feels wonderful. There's a grey haze over there. Hills or mountains, maybe? Storm clouds, perhaps?' She twisted round, shielding her eyes from the sun's glare. 'Is England just one big forest? Wait, I see something . . .'

'What?'

With great care, Hazel braced her knee on the wobbling branch and stood up, clinging to the tree trunk to steady herself.

'Hazel!' Bramley squeaked, his eyes popping open with fright. 'What are you doing?'

'I need a better look.' She pointed to where the forest sloped down into a valley. A river wound through the trees like a silver thread, and beyond rose a column of black smoke.

'That's where we should go,' Hazel said. 'Towards the fire.'

'That smoke is miles off,' Bramley said. 'We're sure to get lost.'

'We won't,' Hazel replied, 'because I have another plan.'

'Oh, joy.' Bramley sighed. 'What is it this time?'

'We follow the moss.'

7
THE WOODSMAN

Anyone found harbouring witches, knowingly or not,
will face the full vengeance of the law.
Amendment to the Witch Laws, passed in 1651

By the time Hazel had scrambled to the ground, the sun was high and the forest streaked with columns of light. Birds chattered all around, fluttering busily in the leaves.

'This way,' Hazel said, and set off through the trees.

'How can you be so sure?' Bramley asked.

'I would have thought a *wise* forest creature like you would know all of nature's secrets,' Hazel said as she hopped over a foaming stream.

'I know what I need to know, and that's enough for me,' Bramley huffed.

Hazel stopped by a gnarled old ash tree. 'Look at the moss on the trunk. Notice anything?'

'No.'

'What about on that one?' she said, pointing to a chestnut tree.

Bramley stared hard. 'Well, there's moss on both of them.'

'Yes, and what does it have in common?'

'It's green?'

'Ye-es. Anything else?'

'Ah! It's only growing on one side.'

'Exactly,' Hazel said. 'Moss only grows on the north side of a tree, and the smoke column is in the same direction. So to get there I'm following the moss. Clever, right? Blind Mary taught me that.'

'Mmm.' Bramley tugged her ear. 'You know, there're other things you need to be doing besides tramping through the forest.'

Hazel hopped over a tree root. 'Like what?'

'Like using your brain. We need to work out *why* that man and his demon took your mother. Tell me about her. What do you know of her life before you were born?'

'Not much.' Hazel frowned. 'She never told me about it.'

'And why did she never let you out of the Glade?'

'I don't know. I asked and asked but she always said I was too young – that she would tell me when the time was right. She was just about to when—'

'Don't you think it's odd?' Bramley said. 'You were trapped, a prisoner, kept away from the world. Why would she do that to you?'

A flash of anger made heat pulse through Hazel's veins. 'Stop asking me questions I can't answer.'

'Perhaps that man and his horrible demon are the reason she created the Glade?' Bramley said. 'Maybe she was just trying to protect you.'

'Maybe,' Hazel replied. 'But she could have trusted me

with the truth. I wish she had. Then maybe we'd have some idea about how to save her.'

Hazel pressed on, mind whirring, stopping only once to rest her aching legs and eat some bread and cheese. By the time she emerged from the forest the sun had set, leaving a bloody smear on the horizon. Freshly cut tree stumps poked sadly through the ground and lopped branches lay stacked in piles. The air smelt of sap and sawdust.

Hazel unslung her bag and perched on a felled tree trunk. 'We did it,' she said, pointing further down the valley. 'Look, we've found a town.'

Huddled in a bend in the river was a walled village. A column of dense black smoke drifted from an open square in the middle.

'I hope there'll be apples there,' Bramley said.

A crown of stars glittered in the pitch-black sky; after the shelter of the forest, Hazel suddenly felt small and exposed. She bit her lip. *Am I ready for this?* she wondered. *I don't know anything about towns or people.*

'Well,' she said at last – as much to Bramley as to herself. 'I supposed we'd better get down there and see what we shall see.'

'I wouldn't if I were you.'

The gruff voice came from behind her. Startled, Hazel leaped to her feet. A man in rough clothes and a hat that shaded his eyes was sitting on the ground with his back against a tree trunk. An axe lay across his lap.

41

'What's the matter?' he said. 'Demon got your tongue?'

'No,' she replied, squaring her shoulders. 'You just startled me.'

'I was watching the sun set.' He tipped back his hat, revealing a haggard face and red-rimmed eyes. 'It's late for a sapling like you to be abroad. What are you doing out here on your own?'

'I'm looking for a friend of mine. I was hoping someone in that town might know where she lives.'

'I'm afraid the troubles of a stranger will not mean much to the people of Watley at the moment,' the man said. 'They have worries and torments of their own.'

'Careful,' Bramley whispered from his hiding place in her hair. 'I'm not sure I like this fellow.'

'Perhaps you could help me then?' Hazel said. 'I'm looking for Mary Applegate. Some call her Blind Mary. She lives somewhere in this forest.'

'Blind Mary, is it?'

'Yes,' Hazel said. 'Do you know her?'

'I do, as it happens.' He stood up, using the axe as a prop. 'But first, I'm going to tell you what has happened to me during these past few days . . . then you might understand why it's dangerous to mention the name Blind Mary to strangers.' He rested his axe on his shoulder and reeled away towards the forest.

Hazel remained where she was, unsure whether to follow him or run away. The stranger's voice floated back through the darkness. 'Come with me, young sapling . . .'

42

'I don't like this at all,' Bramley said. 'Let's just go.'

'No,' Hazel whispered back, plucking him from her curls and hiding him in her cloak pocket. 'We need to hear what he knows about Mary. I'm worried about her.' She followed the man to the door of a wooden cabin on the edge of the clearing.

'Come in,' he said gruffly. 'You've no reason to be afraid of me.'

After a moment's hesitation, Hazel entered a candlelit kitchen, neatly furnished with a stove, table, and a chest of drawers carved with trees and woodland animals. A ladder led up to a loft – the bedroom, she supposed.

'Welcome to my home,' the man said. 'It's not much, but it's the best a humble woodsman can afford.' He opened the stove door and poked at the embers. Firelight glistened on the sweat beading his brow.

'Are you feeling unwell?' Hazel asked.

'Unwell? Oh, yes,' the woodsman said, looking through her with hollow eyes. 'Sick at heart, you might say.'

'We should go.' Bramley's voice was a muffled squeak. 'We might catch whatever ails him.'

Ignoring him, Hazel perched on a stool by the window and clasped her hands in her lap, waiting for the woodsman to continue.

'A Witch Hunter has been plying his trade in Watley,' he said, running a hand down his face.

Hazel tensed. Her mother had sometimes spoken to Mary of Witch Hunters when she didn't think Hazel was

43

listening – they were ruthless men dedicated to finding people accused of wielding magic. *People like me*, she thought, her heart fluttering.

'And not just any Witch Hunter, but Captain John Stearne himself.' The woodsman's voice was flat, like a guilty man confessing his sins. 'They call him "The Butcher". That's who I've been working for.' He pointed at the dresser. 'Pass me the clothes from the top drawer.'

Hazel opened it. Inside were neatly folded dresses: simple clothes, but well made and looked after. She handed them to the woodsman, wondering what he was going to do with them. To her surprise he stuffed them into the stove. Fire raged, casting an orange glow throughout the cabin.

'And what did this man . . . Captain Stearne do?' she asked.

'He came with soldiers to hunt for witches – all kinds, from Wielders to healers.' His face crumpled and tears gathered in his eyes. 'They barred the town gates, trapping everyone inside. Then he set up his court in the market square and judged anyone he suspected of witchcraft.'

Hazel sat unmoving. *I'm beginning to understand why Ma kept me hidden away*, she thought.

'The trials went on for days . . . and when they were over, he ordered me to build the execution pyres.'

'I don't want to hear the end of this,' came a muffled whisper.

Hazel quickly covered her pocket with her hands to stifle Bramley's squeaking – but the woodsman didn't notice, he just gazed into the roaring stove.

Hazel started to tremble. 'So the smoke over the town . . . ?'

The woodsman blinked slowly and nodded. 'Stearne is gone but the pyres still burn. Beacons to show that Watley is cleansed of witchcraft. That is why I am sick in both heart and soul.'

'Who . . . who did they burn?' Hazel whispered.

'Wise women, healers, anyone suspected of having a bit of magic about them, anyone considered . . . odd.' Hazel flinched as his eyes bored into her. 'Women like Mary. She lives somewhere here in Wychwood – no one knows quite where, but the Witch Hunters may have found her. Who knows?' He threw the rest of the clothes in the crackling fire.

Oh no, not Mary, Hazel thought.

'Bottom drawer,' the woodsman said.

Hazel pulled it open and saw more dresses. 'These are children's clothes.'

The woodsman took them from her and clutched them to his chest. 'My wife was a healer,' he said. 'Some said she used magic. Perhaps they were right. And my daughter . . . she looked *so much* like her.'

Hazel watched with dawning horror as he began to feed the clothes into the fire.

'I did what I was told. I would have been killed if I disobeyed,' he said. 'I built the pyres and . . . I had to watch as . . .' His voice trailed away.

Hazel sat in stunned silence until he eventually tore his eyes away from the crackling fire and looked at her.

'Don't go into Watley,' he said. 'Just knowing Blind Mary's name may be enough for someone to denounce you.' His face lit up and he held out the last of his daughter's dresses. 'You could stay here with me. This might fit you. Won't you try it on?'

Hazel shook her head, feeling trapped; the woodman's broad shoulders seemed to fill the cabin, blocking her way to the door.

'I'm sorry for what's happened to you,' she said, as gently as she could. 'But you must let me go.'

'Please stay,' he begged, taking a step forward. 'I can't bear to be on my own.'

Hazel tried to dodge past him but he moved with her. The wild look in his eyes chilled her blood, but she mastered her fear.

'No,' she said, stamping her foot. 'You'll let me go, or you'll be sorry.'

'Please,' he said, then the strength drained from him and he crumpled into his chair.

'I'm sorry, but I really can't stay here with you,' Hazel said, laying her hand on his shoulder.

'Go then, if you must, young sapling.' He reached out and wrapped his fingers around Hazel's hand. 'Go to the gaol in the market square. Find Captain Price and ask him to show you the execution list. If Mary Applegate's name is on it . . . you know that you need look no further for her.

Just remember this: don't tell *anyone* that you're friends with her. Trust no one – *ever*. England is now a place where people betray their own families. Now go.'

Hazel paused by the door. 'What were your wife and daughter's names?' She didn't know why, but she needed to know.

'Rose and Meg. My Rose and Meg.'

'Goodbye,' Hazel said. 'I hope we'll meet again.' She stepped out into the dark and closed the door behind her.

8
A TOWN IN TORMENT

When a Witch Hunter purges a township,
he is allowed to treat the population as he sees fit.
Amendment to the Witch Laws, passed by Parliament, 1646

Hazel picked her way through the clearing. 'That poor man,' she said, releasing Bramley from her pocket and settling him on her shoulder.

'Poor man?' Bramley replied. 'I thought he was going to keep us both prisoner.'

'He was desperate. Couldn't you feel it? It came off him in waves.'

She stroked Bramley's head as she gazed down the valley. Pools of white mist gathered in the deeps and gullies scarring the land. In the distance, a wolf howled. With a deep breath, Hazel settled her bag more comfortably on her shoulder and set off down the hill towards the town.

'You still mean to go there, then?' Bramley said.

'We need to know if Mary's still alive. She's our only hope.'

'Why didn't I just stay in my nest?' Bramley groaned. 'This does *not* feel like a good idea.'

The valley sloped steeply and Hazel had to be careful not to lose her footing on the stony ground. Hardy-looking goats watched her descent until she eventually reached a track running alongside the river. Ahead, the smoke pall stained the sky a dirty grey.

Wattle-and-daub huts with sagging roofs lined the track, and boats bobbed and knocked against rickety jetties. The moon was high and casting a ghostly glow by the time she reached the walls of Watley. The main gate was closed but a side door next to a guards' hut stood open. Inside, a snoring soldier in a tatty red uniform slumped on a stool with his chin resting on his chest.

'Now there's a man who takes his job seriously,' Bramley said.

Hazel crept up to the hut, unhooked the lantern hanging over the door, and passed silently into the town. Two things struck her as she stood in the cobbled courtyard just inside the gate. The first was the overpowering smell of sewage, and the second was the silence.

When daydreaming about the world outside the Glade, she had imagined towns to be busy places full of people, noise, hustle and bustle. Instead, the courtyard and the streets leading from it were deserted, the houses and shops shuttered and dark.

'What's this?' Hazel muttered, kneeling down. The cobblestones were covered in a layer of grey paste. She rubbed it between her fingers.

'I think it's ash and rainwater,' Bramley said, scurrying

49

down to her hand to have a sniff. 'Look, it's everywhere.'

'But where could all this ash be coming from?' Hazel said, before remembering the smoke column and what was causing it. 'Oh.'

'It must have been burning for days,' Bramley said, racing back up to the comfort of her hair.

A dog barked a few streets away, followed by a man shouting. Somewhere behind a nearby shuttered window a woman sobbed. Hazel was gripped with an urge to turn tail and run. *No*, she thought. *I must find Mary. And to do that, I need to talk to this Captain Price.*

Holding up the lantern and avoiding the reeking gutter running down the middle of the cobbles, she set off towards the centre of town using the smoke column as a guide. Empty washing lines hung between buildings like spiders' webs.

Light spilt out from the windows of a tavern; a glimpse inside revealed a low room with tables, chairs and a serving hatch. A few pinch-faced men sat together, talking in low voices. One woman slumped in a corner, red-rimmed eyes staring at nothing.

The road sloped up, passed under a covered butter market and then opened on to an empty moonlit square, fronted on three sides by shuttered houses and shops. Hazel stopped by a horse trough full of brackish water, and knelt down in its shadow.

'Well,' Bramley whispered, 'this place certainly tells a grim tale.'

In the middle of the square were piles of blackened timber, belching smoke, their embers still glowing. Jutting from them were six poles burnt down to charcoal spikes. Ash choked the air, catching in Hazel's throat and making it hard to breathe.

'At least it seems to be over now,' she whispered back. 'Look, there are lights on over there. Perhaps that's the gaol?' She pointed towards a low stone building with a stout door and a rank of barred windows. They were all dark except for one at the end, which glowed with candlelight.

She ducked back behind the horse trough as the gaol door crashed open. Two men in red uniforms ambled out. One dragged his musket on the ground, the other swigged from a bottle.

'Watch out, witches,' the one with the musket slurred. 'The patrol is sallying forth.' Both men folded up, wheezing with mirth.

'Shut your traps, you drunken sops,' bellowed someone from inside the gaol. 'You're militiamen, so act like it or I'll throw you in the cells.'

The men faded into the night. The door slammed shut.

'The local militia,' Hazel hissed. 'Looks like we've found the right place, anyway.'

'I don't think much of their discipline,' sniffed Bramley. 'Are you sure this is a good idea?'

'No, but it's the only one we have.' She took a steadying breath and marched up the gaol steps. There was a piece of parchment nailed to the door:

51

Attention, citizens of Watley,
Your town has been purged.
For the duration, the town militia
(under the direction of the Order of Witch Hunters)
will be enforcing martial law and a strict curfew.
By order of Witch Hunter Captain John Stearne

John Stearne, Hazel thought. *That's who the woodsman talked about*. Standing up as straight as she could, she balled her fist and rapped on the door.

'Come in, if you must,' a voice called. 'It isn't locked.'

Hazel shoved open the door and stepped into a low-ceilinged office. A suet pudding of a man eyed her suspiciously from behind a desk. His frockcoat was under so much strain that the buttons looked about to ping off and ricochet around the room like musket balls.

'Close the door,' he rumbled. 'You're letting the heat out.'

Hazel did as she was told and stood in front of the desk, her mind worryingly blank.

'Well?' he said, scribbling in a ledger with a feather quill that looked tiny clutched between his fat fingers. 'What do you want?'

I'll try being polite, she thought. 'If you please, I'd like to take a look at the execution list.' Not sure what to do next, she dropped a curtsy.

'Would you now?' the man said, laying down the quill and carefully blotting the parchment. 'And why does

52

that blood-soaked list interest you?'

'Well, Mr . . . ?'

'*Captain* Price.'

'Well, Captain Price,' Hazel said, her mind whirring, 'I wish to make sure that the witches I, er . . . denounced received the justice they deserved.'

'Hazel, *really*?' came a squeak from just next to her ear.

Price looked Hazel up and down, pursing his mouth as if he'd eaten something sour. 'One of Stearne's informants, are you? The purge is over. Can't you let the dead rest in peace?'

'No,' Hazel said, trying not to wilt under the man's disgusted gaze. 'I must see it, to put my mind at rest.'

'Too bad. There is no list.' He waved his hand over the paper-strewn desk. 'And there won't be one until I collate all these reports, and that'll take days.' He grabbed a chicken leg from a plate and took a huge bite. 'It's enough to make me lose my appetite.'

'No list?' Hazel said.

'No list,' he repeated, discarding the stripped bone into an upturned helmet. 'Tell me who you denounced – I may well remember their fate.'

Hazel was about to say Mary's name when a terrible thought struck her. *What if Mary survived the purge? What if the Witch Hunters never found her? If I mention her now, they'll be sure to try and hunt her down.* Fluttering with panic, she stared at Price with her mouth still open, trying to think of something to say.

'Well?' he said. 'I haven't got all night.'

'Rose and Meg,' she blurted. 'The woodsman's family. Both witches, I believe.'

'Ah yes. I remember.' Price sighed deeply and rubbed his eyes. 'What a scene that was. Well, you'll be pleased to know that they were the last two people to be executed. Happy now?'

'Yes, sir. I'm glad justice has been served. Goodnight to you.' Hazel's cheeks flushed with shame as she slunk out of the office, closed the door and slumped against the wall.

'So . . . *that* went well.'

'Shut up, Bram,' Hazel hissed.

'Come on, there's no point dwelling on it,' the mouse replied. 'You had to tell him something to keep Mary's name a secret.'

'Did you see the look he gave me?' Hazel's voice was shaking. 'He thinks I'm as bad as the Witch Hunters.'

'Well he's hardly blameless, is he? He and his men helped in this awful business.'

Hazel stamped her foot. 'It was all for nothing. We still don't know what happened to Mary. Or where to find her – *or* Ma.' She held back a sob. 'I just feel so *stupid*.'

'At least you're admitting it now,' Bramley said, tucking himself more firmly into Hazel's hair. 'Oh come on, little witch, don't cry,' he added, hearing Hazel sniff. 'Let's go back to the woods and try and get some sleep. Things will look better in the—'

'Shush,' interrupted Hazel. 'There's someone coming.'

9
MR DAVID DRAKE, WITCH FINDER'S APPRENTICE

'Fire. That's the answer.
Roast 'em down to bones and fat.'
Witch Hunter Captain John Stearne

Bramley ducked behind Hazel's ear just as a boy wearing a pea-green coat, velvet waistcoat and mud-spattered boots materialized out of the darkness. He was striding up the stairs so quickly that he only just stopped in time to avoid knocking Hazel over.

'Evening, miss,' he said, touching the brim of his tricorne hat.

Hazel guessed he was about fifteen – although never having seen a boy before it was hard to tell.

'Er, good evening,' she said, recovering from her surprise.

'I'd get off the streets if I were you,' the boy said. 'It's not safe for a young girl to be wandering about on her own.' Doffing his hat again he dashed up the steps and barged into Price's office. 'Now listen here . . .' he started. The door banged shut.

Hazel backed down the stairs as a crescendo of shouts and crashes drifted through the windows.

'Let's get out of here, before *we* get involved,' Bramley said.

'But I want to see what's going on.'

'Stop being so reckless and—'

Price, red-faced and furious, flung open the door and strode out of the gaol with the boy, sans hat, struggling under his arm. 'The fine to release your master has just doubled,' Price bellowed, hurling the boy down the stairs and kicking his hat after him. 'And don't come back until you have it.'

Hazel stared slack-jawed as the boy jumped to his feet.

'You great, fat *oaf*,' he said, hopping from foot to foot. 'That's my best hat, and how *dare* you manhandle me? Don't you know who I am? You'll be seeing me again and when you do, I'll—'

Price slammed the door and the boy deflated.

'Hello again,' Hazel said.

The boy brushed himself down and tried to apply some shape back to his hat. 'I apologize for the unseemly nature of our reacquaintance but, as you may have noticed, I have just had a disagreement with Captain Lard-Bottom in there.'

'Do you always have that effect on people?' Hazel asked, strangely alert to the boy's cheekbones.

He gave her a lopsided grin. 'I think I just caught him at a bad time.'

Hazel took a step towards him. 'Are you hurt? That was quite a fall.'

'A mere stumble. I'm made of pretty stern stuff, you

56

know. Allow me to introduce myself.' He bowed and threw another smile, which, for reasons Hazel couldn't quite understand, made her heart flutter oddly in her chest.

'Why are you blushing?' Bramley whispered. 'You don't *like* him, do you?'

Hazel ignored him, wishing he'd shut up and let her think.

'My name is David Drake, apprentice to Mr Titus White,' the boy continued, straightening up and jamming his hat back on his head. 'And before you ask, yes, *the* Titus White.'

Hazel looked blank.

'Don't tell me you've never heard of him?' David asked.

'Who's he talking about?' Bramley whispered.

'I'm afraid not,' Hazel said to David. 'Who is he?'

David looked wounded. 'Why, he's only the most celebrated Witch Finder of his generation. I thought everyone had heard of him. I suppose his glory years may be behind him, but still . . .'

'Witch Finder?' Bramley squeaked. 'That's trouble we don't need. Make your excuses and get away. He'll have your head on a spike as soon as he finds out you're a Wielder.'

Hazel knew Bramley was right. This boy who seemed so handsome and charming could well be a killer. She glanced at the smouldering pyres and cold fear ran through her.

'A Witch Finder?' she said, forcing herself to sound enthusiastic. 'How exciting!'

'It can be,' he said, hooking his thumbs into his belt and smiling complacently.

'Travelling around seeking out witches must be very rewarding,' she continued. 'I bet you have loads of interesting tales to tell.'

'Er, yes . . . loads.' His smile wavered.

'He's hiding something,' Bramley whispered.

Hazel agreed. 'Tell me what happened here,' she said, sweeping her arm around the square. 'Did you help to round up witches for this purge?'

'Actually . . . er, no,' he replied. 'A purge like this is government business.'

'Ah,' Hazel replied. 'So what *do* you do?'

David puffed out his chest. 'We are freelance Witch Finders, independent traders, the best in the business. Knights of the road helping those in need.'

'That sounds very impressive,' she said. 'So are you here on business?'

David deflated. 'Well, unfortunately, unforeseen circumstances have made business difficult to pursue.'

'Oh?'

He nodded towards the gaol. 'The boss has got himself arrested again. He's locked up in there.'

'What did he do?' asked Hazel.

'The usual. Got drunk and into a fight.' David sighed. 'He's plagued by dark moods – black dogs, he calls them. They always lead to trouble, and it's always up to me to get him out of it. He's squandered our savings so I can't pay the fine to release him. My father warned me against taking up with Titus, and I'm beginning to see why.'

'Hazel, come on,' Bramley muttered. 'These two sound like a right pair. Take your leave and let's get out of here.'

But Hazel was busy weighing risk against opportunity. A professional Witch Hunter was her mortal enemy, but also someone who might know how to track a demon – which was the best possible way of finding her mother.

'You're about to do something reckless, aren't you?' Bramley hissed from behind her ear. 'I can tell.'

Hazel thought of Hecate in the clutches of the demon. She knew that had it been the other way around, her mother would have stopped at nothing to save her. Taking David's arm, she guided him under the eaves of a smithy.

'Tell me, David,' she said, leaning close and lowering her voice, 'what do you know about . . . hunting demons?'

David's eyes widened. 'The thought of hunting demons was why I became Titus's apprentice in the first place. The fame, the glory . . .'

Hazel gripped his arm tighter. 'Then you've dealt with them before?'

'Not *exactly*.'

She let go of his arm and frowned. 'What do you mean, not *exactly*?'

'Well, I've read a lot about them,' David said.

'You mean you've never even seen one?'

'No – but that's not my fault.' He kicked the ground. 'Freelancers like us haven't been allowed to hunt witches or demons since the war ended. Only Lord Cromwell's official Witch Hunters can do that.'

'Come on, Hazel,' Bramley whispered. 'This boy's no use to us. He wouldn't know a demon if it stood up in his soup.'

As surreptitiously as possible, Hazel gave Bramley a poke to shut him up. 'So if you can't hunt demons or witches, why call yourself Witch Finders?' she asked.

'I told you, before the war Titus was the most famous Witch Finder in the land. But under Cromwell everything's changed. I've been Titus's apprentice for a year now, and do you know what we've been doing in all that time?'

Hazel shrugged.

'Investigating ghost sightings.' He shook his head in disgust. '*Ghost* sightings. The number of nights I've camped out in graveyards as the boss got drunk and fell asleep. And the indignity doesn't end there. *Oh* no! We've sometimes had to stoop to scare-crowing. And me, the son of a duke. No witches. No demons. No glory. And all because the boss won't join the Order of Witch Hunters.'

'Why not?'

'Titus hates Cromwell. Fought against him in the war. The Order wouldn't take him even if he wanted to join.'

'Can't you leave him and go your own way?' Hazel said, trying to ignore Bramley as he nipped at her ear.

David shook his head. 'Of *course* not. The bond between master and apprentice is sacred. If I broke it, I would prove myself to be less than a gentleman. I may be destitute, I may be penniless . . . but I still have my pride.'

'It sounds like you can't help me.' Hazel sighed.

'Now wait a minute,' David said. 'I don't believe this is a

chance meeting. I think providence has thrown us together for a reason.'

'I'm not sure …?' Hazel said, wondering what 'providence' meant.

'I can help you, I promise,' the boy exclaimed. 'Will you give me a chance?'

Hazel looked into his wide blue eyes and something inside her melted. 'Well,' she said at last, 'I suppose I *could* give you a chance.'

'This is a mistake,' Bramley squeaked.

David clapped his hands. 'Marvellous! A proper job at last.' His face turned serious. 'By the way, it's probably best not to mention demons to the boss, for now anyway.'

'Why not?' Hazel asked.

'He's in a fragile state at the moment. The black dog, you know. He might get . . . agitated. I'll ease him into our agreement gently. Just leave him to me. I know how to handle him. Deal?'

This is the right thing to do, Hazel thought, shaking David's hand and noticing how warm his fingers were. *I can't do this on my own.*

'Oh, Hazel,' Bramley moaned. 'What have you done?'

Hazel pretended to scratch her neck and gave him another jab with her finger.

'So now that's settled, you can explain what your problem is,' David said. 'A demon, eh?'

'Be careful how much you tell him,' Bramley whispered. 'Just enough to be useful . . . but not enough to cast suspicion on you or your mother.'

'Yes, a demon,' Hazel said. 'At least I think it was – I'm not an expert like you.'

'Quite, quite . . . Did you see it?'

Hazel nodded.

'So what did it do?'

'It took my mother.'

David's face creased with concern. 'How awful. Tell me what happened.'

'Ma and me live in Wychwood, in a cottage, just the two of us. Two days ago she was washing in the pool and this *thing* . . . came out of the water, grabbed her and dragged her away into the trees.' Hazel looked down at her boots. 'I've been looking for her ever since, but I don't know how to track demons.'

David's frown deepened. 'You're absolutely sure it was a demon? They're very rare. Could it have been a man? Some bandit looking—'

'I know what I saw,' Hazel said.

David nodded. 'It's all right – I believe you.'

'So, will you help?'

'Of course,' David said, laying his hand on her shoulder. 'I am going to dedicate my skills and time to reunite you with your mother, as unharmed as circumstances allow.'

'Thank you,' breathed Hazel, a glow of relief spreading through her.

'Don't mention it. But before we start, you'll need to prepare yourself for the worst. Do you understand what

I'm talking about? Most people who are taken by demons, well . . .'

'She's alive, I know it, and I must find her!'

'And so we shall.' The boy smiled. 'You know I've just realized – I don't even know your name.'

'I'm Hazel. Hazel Hooper.'

'*Well done*,' Bramley hissed. 'Now he knows your real name. So much for subterfuge.'

'What a pretty name,' David murmured. 'Now, as I said, our services are the best value on the market. We ask for a flat fee, plus expenses, all refundable if the venture results in failure. Failure being the, er . . . non-return of your mother.'

Hazel rooted about in her bag and produced the pouch of coins. 'This is all I have.'

'Splendid,' said David, weighing the bag in his hands before handing it back to Hazel. 'Now, first things first – we have to get the boss out of gaol, which unfortunately means dealing with the tubby captain again. But needs must, I suppose. Follow me.' And with that he bounded up the stairs and burst back into Price's office.

Thinking it would have been a good idea to knock, Hazel followed him inside.

10

THE BEAR AND THE SLOP-SPRITE

*'A witch shows neither loyalty nor love;
their hearts are as black as night.'*
Matthew Hopkins, Witch Hunter General

'**Y**ou again,' Captain Price said to David, standing up and planting his knuckles on the desk. 'Do you actually like being thrown downstairs?' Hazel sidled up to the desk and gave the captain her best smile. His frown deepened and he jabbed a greasy finger at David. 'You're not leading this girl astray, are you?'

'He's not, sir,' Hazel said before David had a chance to retort. 'David has agreed to escort me home to, er . . .' Her mind went blank as she realized that she didn't know the names of any other towns.

'Lenham,' David said. 'It's an arduous journey so I'm going to ensure Miss Hooper's safe arrival back into the bosom of her family.'

Hazel slowly let out her breath.

'Well, miss, I'd offer to help you myself, but my lads are busy trying to keep things in order here,' Price said. 'People have been jumpy since the purge. Who knew so many witches lived among us? My washerwoman was found

64

guilty of turning the Red Lion's ale sour. Her own husband turned her in – but then he's a terrible drunk and she was always nagging him to leave off the drinking . . .' He shook his head sadly. 'I don't know who's going to clean my shirts now.'

'We live in dark times,' David said, nodding sagely.

Price glowered at him. 'Miss, I'd warn you against taking up with this troublesome young princeling. Too many airs-and-graces wrapped up in ragged clothes, if you ask me.'

David bristled. 'No one *is* asking you, you lunk-headed—'

Hazel squeezed David's arm. 'Captain, I'd like to pay the fine to release Mr White. Then we can be on our way.'

The chair creaked as Price sat down. 'Titus White, eh? The famous Witch Finder? He was quite a man in his day, but he's a walking wine sack now. I doubt he could find his way to the latrine, let alone Lenham.'

'I shall ensure the young lady gets home,' David said, leaning so far over the desk he was nearly nose to nose with the captain.

Price ignored him and addressed Hazel. 'Drunk as a lord, he was, in the Red Lion. *He* doesn't mind sour ale. Shouting something about a black dog. Took four of my lads to get him into his cell. My uniform got quite rumpled in the fracas.' He smoothed invisible creases out of his frockcoat.

'We'll have him out of your hair in no time.' Hazel passed her bag of coins to Price, who opened it and nodded.

'Don't worry, miss,' he said, handing her an iron key. 'I'll make sure you get your change. White's in the last cell on the left.' He pointed down a dingy stone corridor. 'Yell if he gives you any trouble. Me and the princeling here will finish off the paperwork.'

'The boss'll be fine . . . but he hates rude awakenings,' David called after her. 'Try to rouse him gently.'

The corridor was lit by a guttering torch, and smelt of things Hazel didn't want to think about. Each cell had a heavy wooden door with a barred window. She wondered about the miserable souls who had languished there in the cold darkness over the decades.

She reached the last cell and, standing on tiptoes, peered through the bars. A candle jammed in a bottle illuminated dank walls and a filthy floor. Reeking in the corner was a cloth-covered bucket; the smell made her eyes water. At first she thought the cell was empty, then she noticed a hand poking out from a pile of rags by the wall.

The Witch Finder, she thought with a thrill of apprehension. *Asleep . . . or dead?* She unlocked the door. Hinges creaked in protest as she pushed it open.

'My poor nose,' Bramley squeaked, crawling into the neck of her cloak in an effort to hide from the smell. 'I think I'm going to faint.'

Taking only short breaths through her mouth, Hazel sidled up to the hand, which remained limp and lifeless.

'Titus? Mr Titus White?'

Bending down, Hazel nudged a bulge under the rags that she suspected was a shoulder; then shrieked as the owner of the hand reared up and bellowed like an angry bear. The rags fell away, and she found herself staring up at a man clad in fury and a long black coat.

Before she could speak he grabbed her by the neck and lifted her clear off the ground. Fighting for breath, Hazel kicked and punched with all her might. 'Let . . . me . . . *go*!' she gasped, torn between rage and fear. A burning flash of magic erupted in her heart, but she screwed up her eyes and held it in as best she could.

He mustn't find out I'm a witch, she thought. She could hear Bramley's panicked squeaks from inside the fabric of her cloak and hoped he had the sense to stay hidden. 'I . . . can't . . . breathe . . .'

The man thrust his face close enough for her to see every knot and piece of filth entwined in his wild hair and beard. 'Who in blazes are you? Speak, or I'll shake the teeth out of your skull.' His voice was a rumble that Hazel felt in her chest.

Too stunned to reply – she could only stare into his stone-hard eyes.

'No name, eh?' he barked. 'So where did you come from? Did you spring up from the slop-bucket? Are you a slop-sprite?' He loosened his grip just enough to allow Hazel to reply.

'No,' she eventually managed, choking on the smell of ale and tobacco that seeped from the man's mud-splattered coat. 'I'm your . . . new client.'

The man narrowed his eyes. 'But you're just a *girl*.'

'That may be,' Hazel said, gathering her courage. 'But I'm

also the girl who's bought your freedom . . . and if you don't put me down this . . . *instant*, I'll gladly ask for my money back and leave you here to . . . rot.'

The man's lips peeled back into a snarl.

'Put her down, Boss,' David said from the doorway. 'She's paid the fine and we're free to leave this forsaken town.'

Titus grunted, dropped Hazel and stalked out of the cell.

With as much dignity as she could muster, Hazel brushed herself down and yelled, 'You're welcome,' after him.

'Don't worry,' David said. 'He's always like that when he wakes up.'

II

THE WAGON

'Witches consort with demons, and cast spells,
and other accursed charms and crafts.
It is my duty to fight these evil-doers.'

Pope Innocent VIII

'I'm sorry about the boss. You'll get used to him,' David said. 'Our wagon is just down here.' He led Hazel down an alley and into a dingy courtyard. 'Here we are. Welcome to our perambulating home.'

On the other side of the courtyard was a four-wheeled, enclosed wagon, bathed in the light of two lanterns hooked on to its overhanging eaves. Yoked to the front, drinking from a water trough, were two enormous Clydesdale stallions.

'You live in *that?*' Hazel asked, rubbing at her sore neck. She was relieved to feel Bramley's twitching nose nudging at her fingers from under her cloak.

'We do indeed. It suits the needs of two freelance Witch Finders. It may be small but it has everything we require.'

The horses raised their heads as Hazel approached; she barely came up to their knees. She had never seen horses before and was strangely comforted by their quiet strength and earthy smell. She laughed as one of them

69

whickered and sniffed at her neck.

'Begone, beast!' Bramley yelped.

'What was that noise?' David said.

Hazel froze. 'What noise?'

'A sort of squeaking, like a mouse.' He frowned at her. 'Was it you?'

'I didn't hear anything,' Hazel said, anxious to change the subject. 'Come on, introduce me to your beautiful horses.'

David shrugged. 'Hazel, meet Hercules and Ajax,' he said. 'They seem to approve of you, so that's a good sign. Most of the money we earn goes on their food, but without them we'd be stuck – quite literally. Best horses in England, aren't you, boys?'

Hazel circled the wagon, running her fingers over the flaking red paint. The wood panels and ornate iron edging were pitted and scratched, and in some places had been burned. It looked as if the wagon had been driven through a battle and only just made it to the other side. A crooked chimney issuing smoke poked out from the roof like a mushroom.

The narrow arched windows and grotesque gargoyles leering from each corner gave it the look of a miniature gothic cathedral – albeit one with a dragon-shaped swivel cannon mounted on the roof.

David opened the back door and climbed up the steps. 'Come in; close the door behind you.' He bent down by a pot-bellied stove and gave the embers a stoke. 'You'll soon warm up in here.'

Hazel gawped at the cluttered interior. Lanterns cast a buttery glow on the walls and arched ceiling. Labelled trunks were stacked in piles: 'Tools and Accoutrements', 'Powders and Tinctures', 'Traps and Snares', and one mysteriously called 'Misc'. Half-open drawers overflowed with clothes and blankets.

A barrel stood in one corner, stuffed with rolls of parchment – maps, Hazel guessed – a brace of swords, a musket and a huge soup ladle. On the far wall was a workbench strewn with tools, doubling as a step to a hatch leading out to the driver's seat.

She perched on the lower bunk bed and examined shelves and cabinets filled with books, papers and scrolls. *What a wondrous mess*, she thought, breathing in the smell of woodsmoke and stew.

'Can you see any apples?' Bramley whispered, having settled in his usual place behind her left ear.

Hazel jumped as what she thought was a misshapen pile of hairy cushions in front of the fire turned out to be shaggy dog of indeterminate breed. He opened a brown eye and appraised Hazel in a friendly way before clambering to his feet and giving her a thorough sniff. She endured the examination, mindful that the dog was nearly as tall as she was.

'Don't worry about Samson,' David said, giving the dog a scratch behind the ears. 'He may be as big as a pony, but he's got a heart of gold.' Samson gave Hazel's face an appreciative lick. 'There, see? He likes you.'

A shadow appeared by the door. 'Never mind the dog, boy.' Titus glared at David, his eyes glittering behind a curtain of straggly hair. 'Where the devil's my hip flask?'

'You've only just got out of gaol,' David said. 'Now is not the time for drinking.'

'Hip flask!'

Hazel flinched as Titus banged his fist against the doorframe, causing a painting of a sailing ship to crash to the ground.

'Have you tried your *hip pocket*?' David said with a sigh.

'Don't be a fool. Of course I tried . . .' Titus felt in his pocket and withdrew a battered flask. He downed the contents in one swallow.

'Boss, listen, we've got a job. Paid work.'

'Work? What work?'

David spoke slowly, as if to a child. 'Hazel's mother has been kidnapped by bandits in the forest. She's employed us to find her.'

The furrows on Titus's brow deepened. 'Hazel?' he said. 'Who in the devil's bloody name is Hazel?'

David rolled his eyes.

'I am,' Hazel said, drawing herself up to her full height. 'And you, Mr White, owe me an apology.'

David stared at her, shaking his head ever so slightly. Hazel ignored him, giving the old Witch Finder her fiercest glare.

Slowly, like a bear anticipating a meal, Titus turned his shaggy head towards her. 'Apologize? What the hell for?'

'For strangling me,' she said, cheeks flushing with anger. '*And* calling me a slop-sprite.'

'Don't lose your temper,' Bramley hissed. 'You've got to control your magic. If you don't, we're both for the pyres.'

'You're still breathing, aren't you?' said Titus. 'And you look like a slop-sprite to me.' He held out his hand to David. 'Give me the money.'

'But . . . it's all we have left.'

Titus climbed up the steps and loomed over David, who backed away until he fell into a chair. Despite his age, the old Witch Finder was still strong. 'Money,' he growled.

David poured a few coins into Titus's palm. 'I'm keeping some back,' he said. 'We need to eat as well as drink, you know.'

Titus grunted, pocketed the money and barged out of the wagon.

'The man's a nightmare,' Bramley murmured.

'Is he always like that?' Hazel asked.

'Not *always*,' David replied.

'When will he be back? We need to get moving.'

'He'll be back as soon as he's found something to drink,' David said with a sad smile. He lifted the lid from the stew pot, releasing a rich smell of spiced meat. 'Would you like something to eat?'

Hazel's stomach rumbled despite her anxiety. Her meagre meal in the forest seemed a long time ago. 'Yes, please.'

David ladled stew into two bowls. 'I'm afraid we can

only afford umbles. We've been living on the ragged edge of poverty for too long now. Meals are included in your fee, by the way.'

'Thanks,' she said, taking a spoonful. 'It's pretty good.' They ate in companionable silence. Hazel glanced at David and noticed that he was trying, without much success, to grow a moustache. She smiled as Samson clambered to his feet and laid his huge slobbery head on her lap.

'Urgh! What a dreadful beast,' Bramley whimpered, burrowing deeper into her hair.

Hazel nodded towards a metal contraption propped up on the workbench. It looked like a large soup bowl with delicate brass levers sticking out from the sides. 'What's that?'

David picked it up and set it carefully on his lap. It looked heavy. 'It's one of the boss's inventions. He used to make things like this all the time back in the day.'

'What does it do?' asked Hazel.

David grinned. 'It's a demon trap. We call it the Grinder.'

Hazel looked at the contraption with renewed interest. 'Will we use it to catch the demon that took my mother?'

'It depends. The Grinder can only snare lesser demons – *daemon-minimus* to give them their Latin name. Boggarts, goblins and suchlike. As for bigger demons – Bladecatchers, Gullahtooths – well, they're another matter entirely.'

'Oh,' Hazel said, not really understanding what he was talking about.

'Let me show you how it works.' He pointed to the

levers. 'Every type of demon is unique, so the trap needs to be set correctly for the specific demon you want to catch. You tell the Grinder about the demon – weight, height and disposition – by pressing these levers.'

Hazel leaned closer and saw that the levers were inscribed with words like 'Fat', 'Muscular', 'Scaly', 'Angry' and 'Murderous'.

'Now,' David said, 'when the information is collated we press the "Set Trap" lever.'

'And then?'

'The Grinder releases an aura that the demon can't resist—'

'What's an aura?'

David thought for a moment. 'Well, it's a bit like a smell, I suppose. Imagine the best smell you can think of.'

Hazel thought of the way her mother smelt of flowers after a day tending the garden, and felt tears prickling behind her eyes.

'So the demon senses, or *smells*, the aura and comes running – it can't help itself.' David tipped the contraption up so Hazel could see an array of sharp-toothed cogs inside. 'The demon is snared and pulled inside towards the grinders and then, *splat!* Its mortal body is destroyed and its soul flung back to the demon world. Well, that's the theory anyway.'

'Amazing,' Hazel said, struggling to understand.

'It really is. I wish the boss would teach me how to build such things.'

Hazel put her bowl down. The stew had warmed her stomach and her eyelids drooped. As she surrendered to sleep, she was dimly aware of David guiding her to a soft nest of cushions by the fire and covering her with a blanket.

12
DEMONOLOGY

*The breed of witch known as Wielders are born
with an innate magical talent, which they can
use to great and usually destructive purpose.*
The English Witch Plague *by Jacob Sprenger*

Hazel woke and tried to sit up, but a heavy weight pressed her to the floor. It took a few panic-stricken moments to realize that Samson had fallen asleep on top of her, so she lay still, letting her heart slow down as the dog gently snored.

'He doesn't mind me sharing his bed,' she muttered, untangling herself from his limbs and brushing dog hairs from her dress. 'What a good-natured creature he is.'

'He stinks,' Bramley said from behind her ear. 'I could hardly breathe under there.'

Hazel passed Bramley some berries from her pocket, poured a cup of warm milk from a pan on the fire and sat down at the table. The wagon creaked and swayed like a ship rolling on a heavy sea. Clanging pots and rattling dishes created a cacophonous medley that beat time with every lurch.

I must have been exhausted to have slept through that, she thought.

Titus lay collapsed in sleep, his long legs hanging over the edge of the bottom bunk with one boot on and the other discarded on the floor. In his arms he cradled an empty bottle; the air around him reeked of cider. Hazel gave him a cautious prod with her boot but he didn't stir.

'What a state he's in,' Bramley sniffed. 'Still, we're on the move anyway. It'll be good to leave that awful town behind.'

'David must have set off when Titus got back.' Hazel wrapped the blanket around her shoulders and peeked out of the window. 'I'm glad we met him. I think he'll be able to help us.'

'You're getting gooey-eyed over him.'

'I'm *not* getting gooey-eyed,' Hazel hissed, anxious not to wake Titus.

'I know I'm right because you're angry.'

'Rubbish. It's the opposite. I'm angry because you're wrong – as usual. David's going to help us find Ma and that's all I care about.'

'Oh yes?' Bramley said, leaping on to the table and pointing at the slumbering Titus. 'And what about him? He's nothing but a dangerous liability. A drunken Witch Finder with an evil temper.'

'You're such a nit-picker,' Hazel whispered, refusing to admit that Bramley had a point. 'It's obvious that David's the one who's really in charge.'

'Mmm, well, the boy seems more capable than his master, I'll give you that,' Bramley conceded. 'But you've chosen treacherous allies, Hazel. If they find out you're a witch . . .'

Hazel scooped Bramley up and held him close to her face. 'I know. I'll be careful, all right?'

'You need to be *extra*-careful,' Bramley wagged a claw at her. 'I'll be very angry if I get killed because of you.'

'You're a huge nag for such a small mouse.'

Bramley jumped into her curly red hair. 'I do my best,' came his muffled reply.

Hazel stared out of the window as the wagon rumbled through the darkness. The lantern glow struggled through the whirling fog, lighting up the road and the fields beyond. She was grateful for the fire's warmth; it looked cold outside.

The hatch above the workbench sprang open so suddenly that Bramley barely managed to hide behind Hazel's ear in time. *He's pretty nimble for a portly mouse*, she thought, trying to keep a straight face as his whiskers tickled her neck.

'Ah, you're awake,' David said as he poked his head inside. 'Had a nice sleep? Good. We're out of Watley now and heading for Wychwood. Time for us to get to work.' He pointed to a shelf over Hazel's head. 'There's a book there that might interest you.'

Hazel ran her finger over the leather spines, reading the titles. *A History of Witchcraft; Malleus Maleficarum; Famous Trials and Executions; The English Witch Plague; A Wonderful Discovery of Witches.*

'Some of these books were written by Titus,' she said,

glancing over at the snoring old Witch Finder. '*Spells and Charms – A Study of Benevolent Magic*; *The Trial and Acquittal of the Opperley Witches*; *The Persecution of the Wise and Cunning Throughout History*.'

'I know,' David said. 'Hard to believe he was capable of such a thing, isn't it? I'm afraid you've met him when he's rather past his prime.'

Titus twitched, muttered and rolled on to the floor. There was a moment's silence and then he began snoring again.

'See what I mean?' David said. 'The book you need is called *Demonology* by Theodore Dreisler. It's the big black one with the gold foil, next to *Le Dragon Rouge*. That's the one.' Hazel pulled it off the shelf and nearly fell backwards under the weight. 'Careful, it's heavy. Come on through the hatch and sit next to me. Bring the book.'

Hazel glanced at Titus. 'What about . . . ?'

'Oh, don't worry about him. He'll be asleep for hours yet.'

Hazel handed the book to David, gave Samson a goodbye scratch behind the ear, then clambered through the hatch and sat down on the driver's seat. Her breath misted in the air. Bramley curled up at the nape of her neck, radiating heat. She pulled an apple out from her bag and offered it to David.

'Hey,' Bramley squeaked. 'That's *mine*!'

'No, thank you. I can take or leave apples,' David said. 'Now, if what you saw really was a demon—'

80

'I've told you – it was.'

'Then perhaps you'd like to look through *Demonology* and see if you can identify it?'

Hazel laid the book on her lap. The smell of foxed paper wafted out as she opened the front cover. A piece of parchment framed with gold had been stuck to the front page:

To Captain Titus White,
England's Greatest Witch Finder and true Knight of the Road
With thanks from His Royal Highness
King Charles
Charles R.
Patron of the College of Witch Finders

Hazel hoisted the book up and pointed to the page. 'Titus met the King?'

'He *worked* for the King. Titus was one of his closest courtiers,' David said. 'But that was before the Witch War and the King's execution.'

Hazel didn't want her ignorance of what was probably common knowledge to arouse David's suspicion, so she dropped the subject and read on. The title page was printed in a bold gothic font:

𝔇𝔢𝔪𝔬𝔫𝔬𝔩𝔬𝔤𝔶
𝔟𝔶 𝔗𝔥𝔢𝔬𝔡𝔬𝔯𝔢 𝔇𝔯𝔢𝔦𝔰𝔩𝔢𝔯
𝔄𝔩𝔩 𝔨𝔫𝔬𝔴𝔫 𝔡𝔢𝔪𝔬𝔫𝔰, 𝔦𝔪𝔭𝔰, 𝔰𝔭𝔦𝔯𝔦𝔱𝔰 𝔞𝔫𝔡 𝔰𝔭𝔯𝔦𝔱𝔢𝔰 𝔞𝔯𝔢

contained herein, with comprehensive notes and illustrations.

Only the King, the Privy Council and members of the College of Witch Finders are allowed to read the contents of this book.

On pain of death.

Intrigued, Hazel turned the page and saw a picture of a hideous creature, carefully outlined in black and coloured with delicate ink washes.

'Beautiful penmanship, isn't it?' David said. 'Dreisler was a genius. The way he made such ugly creatures look so luminous. Marvellous.'

Hazel didn't think the frog-like creature with the bloated throat looked luminous; she thought it looked terrifying.

The heading on the page – *Shabriri – daemon-minimus* – was followed by some introductory text: *Shabriri are mischievous toad-like demons that wait near uncovered water. They strike blind and eat those that drink of the water.*

She turned the page. A beast with crooked horns and a scorpion's tail grinned at her. *Azazal. Daemon-mediocritas. An insidious demon that invades the hearts of the virtuous, turning their will to its own ends.*

Fascinating, frightening, but not the demon she was looking for. 'Where are we going?' she asked as she leafed through one page of horrors after another.

'We need to pick up the demon's trail as soon as we can.

Can you direct us to where the abduction took place?'

'No, you can't,' Bramley whispered. 'That horrible hedge is in the way, remember?'

He's right, Hazel thought. *Besides, how can I explain that I spent all my life until yesterday living in a magical Glade protected by an enchanted hedge?*

After a moment's thought, she said, 'I'm not sure I can. I got lost in the forest and I don't think I can find my way back.'

'Pity,' David said with a frown.

'Ma never let me go far alone because of Boggarts and wolves and suchlike. So I don't really know my way around.'

'Never mind, I'm here to help now,' David said with an indulgent smile. 'If you can identify the demon, we can try to work out where he's most likely to be hiding. Keep looking.'

Flushed with relief, Hazel continued to turn the pages.

'You and your mother lived alone in the forest?' David asked.

'Yes, just the two of us.'

'A hard life to choose. It must have been lonely.'

'No, not really. We had each other. And a few friends too,' she added hurriedly, thinking of Mary and hoping she was safe.

'Careful, Hazel.' Bramley squirmed his way closer to her ear. 'Remember *what* David is. Don't give too much away.'

'And what of your father?'

David's voice was light, but Hazel heard the curiosity in

it. Bramley was right – she needed to be careful.

'He's dead,' she said, surprised at how easily the lie came to her. 'Killed in the war. I never knew him.'

'The Witch War?' David said, looking sidelong at her. 'Interesting. Did he side with the King and his witches, or Lord Cromwell?'

Hazel felt as if she was walking on a tightrope. One false move and she'd topple to her death. She decided to hedge her bets. 'I'm not sure,' she replied, as smoothly as she could. 'Ma never spoke about it. She always said the subject was far too painful.'

David nodded and squinted up the dark road.

She turned the next page and started in surprise. It was a picture of a demon, *the* demon, *her* demon, crook-backed and skinless. Caught in the light of the swinging lantern the image seemed to swell, as if drawing breath. Gripping the book to stop her hands from shaking, she read on:

> *Rawhead. Daemon-mediocritas. Blind, but with a keen nose for magic, making it ideal for hunting witches. It resides in the Slaughter Gardens of Dryhthelm, the dreaded demon Underworld, and always carries with it the stench of blood.*

If it can smell magic, does that mean it can smell me? Hazel thought. *Perhaps the smell of the enchanted hedge hid my scent back there in the forest? Next time I might not be so lucky.*

'I've found it,' she said, passing the book to David.

'Excellent. Take the reins, would you? Don't worry, the horses will walk on.' He frowned at the picture. 'Are you sure this is the one? It's a *daemon-mediocritas* – which means it's in the mid-ranks of the demon hierarchy. It would take a Wielder of enormous skill to summon it and keep it bound.'

'I know what I saw,' Hazel said, her voice shaking. 'If we're going to work together you need to trust me.'

'All right, I believe you. It's just unusual, that's all.' David scratched his chin. 'You know, I'd prove myself to be a Witch Finder to be reckoned with if I captured a *daemon-mediocritas*.'

'I'm paying you to help find my mother, not improve your reputation.'

'I know, I know,' David said hurriedly. He took another look at the picture. 'I'd better tell the boss about this. This demon is too much to handle on my own.'

'Shall I wake him?' asked Hazel.

'Probably best to wait until he wakes up, er . . . naturally,' David advised. 'Don't worry. I'll look after you.'

Hazel bristled. 'I don't need looking after. What I *do* need is to know how we're going to find this horrible creature.'

David tapped his nose. 'We Witch Finders have our methods.' He reached back inside the hatch and retrieved a polished wooden box. 'Take a look in there,' he said, handing it to Hazel and taking back the reins.

Hazel opened it. Nestling in the frayed, red velvet

lining was a pair of silver goggles, with thick glass lenses and a leather strap. Each eyepiece had several adjustable focusing wheels and brass levers etched with writing. Hazel lifted them up and was surprised by how heavy they were.

'What are these for?' she asked.

'Hunting demons, of course,' David said with a grin. 'The boss designed them himself.'

'How do they work?' Hazel fiddled with one of the rotating wheels. It clicked solidly as she turned it.

'Well, when a demon is summoned from Dryhthelm – that's where demons come from – they begin to decay.' He took the goggles from her and adjusted some of the wheels. 'For a demon like Rawhead, being in our world is a slow and painful death sentence.'

'You mean he might already be dead?'

'I doubt it. It would take a long time for a demon like Rawhead to wither away – and there are ways they can prolong their existence in our world.'

'Like what?' asked Hazel, both fascinated and horrified.

'They feed.'

Hazel's stomach churned. 'On what?'

'Animals . . . people . . . whatever they can find – as long as it's fresh. They're particularly partial to children.'

'Ask him about dormice,' Bramley squeaked.

'The advantage for us is that the decaying demon leaves a trail behind,' continued David.

'Like a slug?' asked Hazel.

'Almost exactly!' He put the goggles around Hazel's head and adjusted the strap to fit. Hazel tried to stifle a giggle as she felt Bramley wriggling his way under the neck of her cloak to avoid David's clumsy fingers.

'Demon trails are invisible to the naked eye,' David went on, 'but that's where these Entropy Goggles come in handy. Comfortable?'

Hazel nodded, the weight of the goggles making her head feel unbalanced. 'But I can hardly see—'

'I've adjusted them to show Rawhead's trail. Everything else will be indistinct.'

Hazel pushed the goggles up her head and blinked her eyes back into focus. 'How long do the trails last?'

'It depends on the demon. A lesser demon's trail – a Boggart's, for instance – may only last a few hours, whereas a more powerful demon leaves a more indelible one. The boss says you can still see traces of a greater demon summoned by a Grand Magus in the Hebrides, and that was five hundred years ago in eleven sixty-three.'

'What about . . . Rawhead?' Even saying the name brought the taste of blood to Hazel's mouth.

David tapped the cover of *Demonology*. 'Our chap is of middle rank. I'd say his trail could last for several days.' He shook his head in wonder. 'A *daemon-mediocritas*. This could be the making of me.'

Hazel closed the book, shutting her nemesis away. The fields on either side surrendered to rocky scrubland dotted with a few stunted bushes. A stream bubbled somewhere in the darkness. She peered ahead as a dark shadow grew from the fog.

Wychwood, she thought with a thrill of fear. *Where the demon might be.*

13

SILK AND POISON

'The King is defeated. The Witch War is over.
It's time to exterminate the rats.'
Lord Protector Oliver Cromwell

T he wagon rocked and creaked its way into the forest. A pair of hanging metal cages guarded the entrance, each gibbet containing a crumbling skeleton shrouded in rags. A raven sat hunched on a wrought-iron 'C' at the top of one of the cages.

'C for Cromwell,' David remarked. 'Odd to think that there used to be witches in the King's court, isn't it?'

'It certainly is,' Hazel hazarded.

'Things are very different now, of course. It won't be long before there are no witches left in England at all. Then all of us ordinary folk will be safe from them forever. Cromwell says the witches who remain at large will do anything to get revenge for losing the Witch War.'

Hazel looked sidelong at David. 'Are there many witches left now?' she asked.

David shook his head. 'Very few, I should think. The Witch Hunters under General Hopkins have seen to that. Most have gathered in the North, but Lord Cromwell himself is leading his army to defeat them.' He sighed. 'I wish I was up there with him.'

The forest closed in, branches lacing together to shut out the sky. Only a few streaks of moonlight reached the road. The gloom dampened even David's spirits. Only the horses seemed unperturbed as they plodded down the rutted track, their perspiring flanks steaming in the cold. Hazel eventually got used to the wagon's sway, her backside becoming so numb that she couldn't feel the seat. Sleep stole over her.

Perhaps it was a drop in temperature or a shift in wind direction that woke her up and quickened her heart; she knew Bramley felt it too because he stirred and shivered, his bristling whiskers tickling her neck.

'David?' she said.

'Mm?'

'Can you . . . *feel* something?'

David nodded towards the gnarled trees encroaching on the road. 'The mist is getting worse,' he said. 'Is that what you mean?'

Sure enough, fog was seeping through the trees on either side, filling the shadows with grey vapour. The first white tentacles were already uncoiling on to the road in front of them. Hazel tasted moisture in the air and water droplets gathered on her cloak. She peered ahead at a dark shape lying prone across the road.

'Stop the cart,' she hissed. 'I see something.'

'Whoa, boys.' David pulled on the reins and the wagon

90

creaked to a stop. 'It looks like a body.' He reached under his seat, pulled out a short wooden club and climbed down the ladder. 'You stay here. If there's trouble, get the boss.'

'But you said not to wake him up,' Hazel said.

David shrugged. 'Just don't get within arm's reach. Try shouting "fire". Actually, "ale" will probably do the trick.'

Hazel perched anxiously on the edge of her seat as David crept up the side of the road towards the shape. His boots crunched on the ground.

'Can you smell something odd?' Bramley asked, squirming out of Hazel's hair and on to her shoulder.

Hazel sniffed. *Could it be . . . ?*

She lowered the Entropy Goggles over her eyes. The world faded and was replaced by blurry shapes. The only thing in focus was a trail of glowing red footprints leading out of the forest, around the body and then snaking down the road into the distance.

'Rawhead,' breathed Hazel. 'He's been here . . .'

'I have a bad feeling about this, Hazel,' squeaked Bramley.

David stopped a few feet from the body and crouched down, head cocked. Through the goggles he was nothing more than a shimmering wraith. 'She's alive,' he called. 'I can see her breathing.'

Hazel ripped off the goggles just as something shifted in the branches over David's head. A shower of leaves drifted down.

'David,' Hazel shouted, feeling the tremor in her voice. 'Come back!'

He turned to her. 'What?'

'Come back, *right now.*' She pointed at the drooping branches. 'There's something—' Her voice seized up in her throat.

David looked up. Above him hung a huge spider; at least twice the size of a grown man. Moonlight drowned in its bulging eye-clusters. Silver venom dripped from its fangs. Eight legs, splayed like an open hand, reached towards him.

'David!' Hazel screamed.

For a frozen moment the spider and David stared at one another; then the creature dropped on a glistening length of silk, smothering him before he could make a sound. Through the hideous tangle of legs, Hazel saw the spider work its fangs into David's cheek.

With a violent spasm, he flopped to the ground like a boned fish and lay perfectly still.

14
LILITH AND SPINDLE

Nicolas Murrell spent many years studying
demons, and is an expert in their evil ways.
A Contemporary Study of Witches by William Steer

Hazel pressed her back against the wagon as the spider turned its bulbous eyes towards her. She felt as if it had caught her in an invisible web; all she could do was watch as it sidled towards her, its long hairy legs stroking the ground.

'We've got to wake the Witch Finder,' Bramley squeaked, scrambling around her hair in a panic.

A spark of hope ignited in Hazel's chest as the woman in the road rose to her feet and sidled towards the spider. Something long and metallic glinted in her hand.

Stab it, Hazel thought. *Save us all!*

The woman was level with the spider's back leg when she looked up and smiled. 'Hello, Hazel,' she said in a voice as light as snow. 'Thank goodness we've found you. Please don't be frightened of Spindle; she won't harm you.'

'Who . . . ? How do you know my name?' Hazel gasped.

The spider flattened its abdomen and shuddered with pleasure as the willowy young woman ran the silver comb through its bristles.

'We know all about you. We've been looking everywhere for you.' The woman tucked her long, dark hair behind her ears and took a step forward. Her skin was so white is seemed to glow. Spindle followed, front legs tickling the air.

Hazel stood up with her fists clenched. 'Stay where you are – don't come any closer.'

The woman stopped and tucked the comb into her shawl. 'It's all right, I'll stay here. I'm a Wielder, like you. My name is Lilith, the last Frost Witch in England.' She held up her bare arms, smiling as white mist poured from her skin and gathered in swirling eddies at her feet. 'Don't be afraid, I'm here to help.'

'I definitely think we should be afraid,' Bramley said. 'That creature she's with isn't natural . . . It's a demon, I'm sure of it.'

'What's your horrible spider . . . *thing* done to my friend?' Hazel said. 'He's not moving. If you've killed him, I swear . . .' she trailed off. *Swear what? What can I possibly do?*

'She told us you had a fiery spirit,' Lilith said. 'I can see it now. It matches your hair.'

'Who told you?'

A frown cut a furrow in the witch's flawless brow. 'Why, your mother, of course.'

Hazel gawped at her. 'My . . . mother?'

'She's lying, Hazel,' squeaked Bramley. 'Don't listen to her.'

'Yes. We found her lost in the forest. She was badly hurt. *Burned.*'

Dread punched Hazel in the stomach as she remembered the wave of fire she had cast back at the pool.

'Don't worry.' Lilith held up a hand. 'She'll recover. *We're* looking after her now.'

Hazel distrusted her relief as much as she distrusted the witch. 'Who's "we"?' she asked.

Lilith took a step forward. Hazel saw that her eyes were as cold and clear as a frosty morning. 'Friends,' she said. 'Witches. People like you.'

'Me and my mother don't need friends – we have each other.'

'If that's true, then what are you doing consorting with a Witch Hunter?' Lilith gestured contemptuously at David's crumpled figure.

'He said he'd help me—'

'Help you?' Lilith shook her head sadly. 'Do you know what he'd do if he found out what you are? He'd kill you –' she snapped her fingers – 'just like that.'

Hazel stamped her foot. 'You don't know that for sure.' Fire flickered in her hair.

Lilith held both hands up, palms outward. 'Hazel, please believe me—'

'No. You're a liar,' Hazel said, her voice low. 'Now let us pass or you'll regret it. I'm going to take David and find my mother.' She jumped as a deep voice rolled like thunder through the shifting mist.

'I'm afraid I can't let you do that.'

Lilith lowered her head and Spindle cringed.

'Who's this now?' Bramley whispered, his claws pricking Hazel's neck.

Hazel felt her magic seep away like water through her fingers. 'Trouble,' she replied.

15
NICOLAS MURRELL

'Curses, poisons and plagues are their weapons.
Beware the witch. They live among us.'
Father Alfred Jourgensen

A man wearing a cloak of black feathers and resting a walking stick on his shoulder strode out of the fog. 'Cold as a grave tonight, isn't it?' he said, stopping in front of the wagon and leaning on his stick. His face was shrouded in a deep hood, but the lanterns flashed on dark eyes that peered keenly at Hazel.

The man from the forest.

'Get out of my way,' Hazel said.

The man raised his hands. 'I just want to talk to you.'

'I won't do anything until I see David,' she said.

'The boy is fine. Spindle just put him to sleep, that's all.'

'Why should I believe you?' Hazel said, gripping the seat so hard she thought it would snap.

'I am not a liar, Hazel Hooper. Nor am I a murderer.' His smooth voice oozed into her mind like syrup, calming her nerves and soothing her fear.

This isn't right, she thought. *Why do I want to believe him?*

97

'Don't listen,' Bramley muttered. 'He's lying, just like that witch.'

Hazel shook her head, trying to clear her thoughts. 'You might not be a murderer, but you did take my ma,' she said. 'I saw you by the Border Hedge.'

'Did you now?' He reached out and stroked Hercules's nose. 'Your mother told me you were clever, and I see that she was right. Very well, let us talk honestly to each other.'

Why do I feel like I'm the dishonest one? Hazel tried to keep hold of the truth but it had become slippery in her mind.

'Let me relieve you of the one fear that I know weighs you down,' he continued, raising his finger into the air. 'The one thing that stands between us. The one thing that is stopping *us* from becoming *friends*.'

Hazel felt fuzzy, as if his words were sticking to her brain and clogging it up. She stared at his hovering finger, vaguely aware of Bramley squeaking into her ear, but the mouse's words were slurred and meaningless.

'Your mother, Hecate, is safe and well in my care,' he said. He lowered his finger and Hazel was engulfed by a wave of relief and gratitude. But a part of her deep inside knew that this outpouring of emotion was false, and that her sudden, inexplicable trust in this man was misplaced.

She wobbled to her feet, mind churning. 'Who are you?'

'My name is Nicolas Murrell, and I have the honour of leading the Chosen. Have you heard of us?'

Hazel ran her hand over her face. She felt woozy, and

when she spoke her voice sounded far away. 'No. Who are the Chosen?'

'The Chosen is a secret organization of witches and Wielders, good people like my consort, Lilith here –' the witch bowed her head and smiled – 'sworn to end the oppression of our kind.'

'You took my mother . . .'

Murrell nodded. 'That's true, and I'm sorry for it, but we need her and the power she wields. We didn't mean for her to get hurt. That, I'm sorry to say, was *your* fault.'

An image of Hecate's terrified face flashed into Hazel's mind, cutting through the confusion. A spark of anger kindled in her stomach. 'Your demon grabbed her. It *hurt* her . . .'

Bramley's squeaking became louder and more insistent, stabbing through the fug inside her head.

'No, Hazel,' Murrell said. '*You* hurt her. With your fire-magic. My demon was trying to protect her.'

'No . . .' Hazel shook her head and the world spun. She wasn't sure of anything any more.

Murrell took a step closer. 'But she forgives you, Hazel, and she wants to see you again. I made a promise to bring you back to her. You don't want to disappoint your mother, do you?'

No, I don't want to disappoint Ma. Hazel stood up. 'I just want to see her again.'

'Hazel, listen to me,' Bramley's voice pierced her mind like a needle. 'He's *lying*.'

Murrell offered a hand towards her. 'Come. Leave the dangerous company of this Witch Hunter and join your own people. Don't you want to see your mother again?'

Hazel longed to feel her ma's arms around her and hear her soft voice telling her that everything was going to be all right. She moved to the ladder as if in a dream.

'Hazel!' Bramley wailed.

She looked at Murrell's outstretched hand and put her foot on the top step.

At that moment David stirred and struggled to his knees. His face was pale and oddly bloated. 'Don't leave, Hazel,' he cried. 'They'll kill me.'

Murrell's head whipped round towards him. 'Spindle,' he snapped.

The spider hissed and sprang back towards David, sinking its fangs into his cheek.

Hazel blinked. Her mind cleared. Murrell's spell was broken. The silken words he'd implanted in her mind shrivelled up in the rising flames of her anger. She stepped away from the ladder and leaned over the railing as the spider-demon scuttled away from David's motionless body and started to advance towards her.

'You're a liar,' she shouted. 'You stole my ma and poisoned my friend.'

'Hazel,' Bramley cried from somewhere near her shoulder. 'I thought I'd lost you.'

Murrell looked disappointed. 'Your mother wouldn't want us to fight, Hazel.'

'That shows what *you* know,' she replied. 'Because fighting you is *exactly* what she'd want me to do.' Heat rose in a haze from her skin.

Murrell took a few steps back, gesturing for Lilith and Spindle to do the same. 'Before you strike me down,' Murrell announced, 'let me give you some advice.'

Hazel hardly heard him over the rush of blood in her ears; her chest glowed like a furnace as she gathered her magic.

'Never,' Murrell continued, 'start a battle without knowing the odds.' He glanced over his shoulder and shouted, 'Rawhead!'

Fear suffocated Hazel's fire and she shrank back against the wagon as the demon stalked out of the mist – powerful, menacing and cloaked in blood-stink. It halted by Murrell, leaning forward on its knuckles, nostrils dilated, and pointed its blank face towards her.

Murrell placed his thumb-less hand on the creature's head.

It can smell me. Just like the book said. Hazel tried to swallow her fear but the demon's ravaged flesh and rows of teeth melted her courage away. It pawed the ground, carving runnels in the dirt.

'Steady, Rawhead,' Murrell said. He turned to Hazel. 'I'm afraid you've made quite an enemy of him.'

'I'm glad.' Hazel wished her voice wouldn't shake so much.

'Did you know that in our world, demons cannot heal their wounds? Rawhead is in great pain from the burns you gave him.'

'Well, I'm *so* sorry,' Hazel said. 'Remind me to be more welcoming next time a demon comes to abduct my mother.'

'This is your last chance.' Murrell pointed his walking stick at her. 'I don't want to hurt you, but I will if you force my hand.'

'You can't fight us all,' Lilith added as she sidled closer, her oversized spider-demon behind her.

Hazel raised her arms and flames spread from her hands like a phoenix reborn. 'I can try.'

Murrell, Rawhead, Lilith and Spindle spread out in a semi-circle and began to close in on the wagon. The horses shied anxiously, jingling their harnesses.

Can I do this? Can I deliberately hurt other people? Hazel thought. A worm of doubt wriggled in her stomach.

That half-second of hesitation was all Murrell needed. He slammed his walking stick on to the ground and a blinding light flashed from the handle. Hazel yelped in surprise, and through the rain of stars obscuring her sight, she saw Lilith bounding towards her, closely followed by Spindle.

Hazel cast her arm towards them and released her magic. A wild arc of fire roared from her fingers, lighting up the forest and scouring the ground to the side of the wagon. The horses reared backwards in panic, almost jerking Hazel off her feet as smoke filled the air and flames cut a swathe across the track, throwing up dirt and vaporizing puddles.

'Lilith!' Murrell dropped his stick and dived forward, throwing his arms around the witch's waist and knocking her away from the wave of fire. She screamed as they landed together and rolled to a stop at the edge of the track.

Murrell lay on his back, the edge of his cloak smouldering from where the flames had caught him. 'Get the girl,' he growled to Rawhead.

Hazel slumped into the seat, blinking the sight back into her eyes, vaguely aware of Samson barking frenziedly inside the wagon.

Rawhead appeared through the receding wall of fire, vaulting from the back of the whinnying horses and up on to the carriage. The wagon creaked under its weight.

Clammy, long-fingered claws closed around Hazel's neck, shoving her back against the wagon and cutting off her breath. She stared past rows of teeth into the ridged flesh on the roof of Rawhead's mouth. The smell of blood was overwhelming.

'Rawhead,' Murrell cried. 'Don't kill her – I command you *not to kill her.*'

The demon leaned closer, mouth widening. Hot breath blasted her skin.

A roar came from inside the wagon, followed by a crash as a roof hatch was thrown open. Everyone froze. Rawhead's grip loosened just enough for Hazel to strain her head towards the noise.

Titus White appeared through the hatch, coat billowing and with a blunderbuss in his hands. He glowered at them all from under a wide-brimmed capotain hat.

'So,' he bellowed, 'what the *hell* do we have we here?'

16

THE WITCH FINDER

Cromwell's Witch Hunters have rejected the dead King's
Witch Finders' principles of investigation, fairness and justice,
and replaced them with brutality, indifference and fear.
England – A Land in Turmoil by Lady Lucinda Munday

The stooped drunkard last seen snoring on the floor and stinking of cheap cider had gone. Titus White now glared down at them all like a preacher berating his terrified congregation from a pulpit.

The demon snorted, its claws still tight around Hazel's neck.

Titus flicked his eyes at her. 'Slop-sprite,' he said with a sharp nod. Then the blunderbuss roared, spewing fire, metal shards and a plume of black-powder smoke.

Hazel gasped a lungful of sulphur-tinged air and fell back into the seat, cracking her head against the eaves and dislodging Bramley who tumbled out of her hair with a terrified squeal and landed on the footboard.

The demon lay on the ground, mouth agape and seeping blood. Its neck and shoulders were covered with smoking shrapnel wounds. Quick as she could, Hazel grabbed Bramley and put him in her pocket.

'Rawhead – get up.' Murrell's cry cut through the fading

echoes of the gunshot. 'Kill the man, but leave the girl unharmed.'

To Hazel's horror, the demon was already lurching back to its feet, turning its blank, eyeless face towards her. Murrell, mud-splattered and shaking with anger, stalked behind it, his face still hidden by his hood.

'This is Rawhead, blood-hunter, prince of the Slaughter Gardens in the seventh circle of Dryhthelm. Did you really think your wretched little pop-gun would stop him?' he yelled at Titus.

Ajax and Hercules stamped nervously as Lilith and Spindle edged forward from the roadside. Trapped inside the wagon, Samson continued his barrage of fearsome barks.

'That was just a warning shot,' Titus growled, dropping the blunderbuss and reaching for the swivel cannon. Hazel groped for the reins, preparing herself for what she guessed was about to happen.

Murrell stopped and pointed his stick at Titus. 'Wait,' he breathed. 'I know you. Damn me to the devil, I *know* you.'

Titus curled his lip and aimed the cannon at Murrell. 'No one knows me any more,' he said, and pulled the trigger. The flint struck the firing pan with a *click*. Nothing happened. No one moved, then Titus yelled, 'Misfire! Drive, girl, *drive*.'

Hazel jerked the reins. 'On, on!' she cried as the horses pulled away, their iron-shod hoofs ringing on the road as they picked up speed.

Bramley scrambled up her dress and perched behind her ear. 'Go on, Hazel, run that beastly man down.'

Murrell stood transfixed in the wagon's path, staring at Titus as if he couldn't believe who he was seeing. The half-panicked horses bore down on him, snorting and tossing their great heads.

Hazel braced herself, waiting for the snap of breaking bones but a second before impact, Rawhead leaped full-stretch and pushed Murrell to safety. The wagon rumbled past, the front wheel clipping Rawhead's tail as it tumbled into the ditch next to Lilith and Spindle – its master clutched in its arms.

Ahead, David lay prone in the middle of the road.

'Titus, can you grab him?' Hazel yelled, her voice nearly drowned out by jangling reins and creaking axles.

'Drive around him, I'll do the rest.'

Hazel pulled the reins and the horses jinked left. She slid helplessly across the polished seat as the wagon slewed off the road, spraying dirt into the air; for a breathless moment she thought it would capsize.

Titus swung his legs over the railing, clambered down from the roof and dropped on to the running board just behind the driver's seat. The wagon juddered over the rough ground at the side of the road, but somehow the old Witch Finder kept his balance as he crouched down with one arm outstretched.

'Slow down,' he commanded.

Hazel pulled back on the reins. As the horses slowed to a trot Titus grabbed David by his trouser belt. 'Go, go!' he grunted to Hazel as he lifted the boy off the ground and, using the wagon's momentum, swung him on to the seat next to her. Hazel jerked the reins with one hand and grabbed David's collar with the other.

Titus clambered into the seat after him, breathing hard. Amazingly, his hat was still perched on his head. 'Get us back on the road before the wheels come off.'

Hazel glanced at David as she steered the wagon off the verge. One side of his face was horribly swollen. His right eye was lost deep in folds of flesh, the other open and unseeing. She reached towards the bite wounds on his cheek, hoping to stop the flow of blood.

'Don't touch him,' Titus snapped. 'Do you want to get poisoned too?'

'Will he . . . ? Is he going to—?'

'Die? I don't know. I'm taking him inside.' He glanced back up the road. 'I can't see anyone following. Keep driving – and keep the pace up. We'll talk when I've seen to the boy.'

Hazel nodded and geed the horses along as Titus clambered through the hatch, dragging David after him. When he closed the door, Bramley crept out of Hazel's hair, scurried down her arm and perched on her lap.

Hazel laid a hand on him. 'You're shaking.'

'Of course I'm shaking,' he squeaked. 'I'm terrified.'

'David looked terrible,' she said. 'His face is all . . . bloated.'

'It's not your fault.' Bramley nudged Hazel's fingers with his nose.

'It *is* my fault.' The horror of it all made her feel sick. 'If he dies . . .'

'Listen,' Bramley said. 'You need to think fast. The Witch Finder is going to ask what was going on back there—'

Hazel jumped and Bramley scrambled into her cloak pocket as the hatch crashed open. Titus thrust out his head, now minus the hat.

'Slow down, slop-sprite,' he said, climbing out, 'or the horses will drop dead from exhaustion.'

Hercules and Ajax snorted as she reined them in to a trot, their heaving sides streaked with sweat.

Bramley's right, Hazel thought to herself. *I've got to get my story straight or I'll wind up on the end of a rope.*

'How is he?' she asked.

'Dying.' Titus grabbed the reins from her. 'Just what bloody story have you written us into, girl?'

'I'm looking for my ma. I asked David to help me find her, that's all.'

'By God, that's *not* all. Accosted by demons and Wielders in my own wagon? And my mooncalf apprentice nearly killed? What in blazes happened back there?'

'They were waiting for us. There was a woman in the road, so David went to see . . . to help. Then that huge spider . . .'

'That idiot boy walked into an ambush? I thought I'd taught him better than that.'

'Well, where were *you*?' Hazel cried. 'Laid out drunk and no good to anyone, that's where.' She yelped in surprise when he grabbed her chin and thrust his face close to hers.

'Lucky for you I woke when I did. That demon had a

108

fierce hankering for your flesh.' He cocked his head, granite-hard eyes boring into her.

He knows, she thought, dread rising in her stomach. *He knows what I am!*

'But its handler,' Titus continued. 'The hooded man – he wanted you alive. Why would that be, I wonder?'

'I don't know,' Hazel almost sobbed with fear. 'I'm just a girl . . . looking for her mother.'

'Just a girl,' Titus muttered. 'I don't believe that for a greased second.'

'He said he knew you,' Hazel gasped. 'Do *you* know who he is?'

Titus let go of her face and Hazel leaned away, trembling. 'There was something familiar about him,' he murmured, stroking his beard. 'But right now we have bigger problems.' He jerked a thumb back down the road. 'They'll be after us, no doubt about that.'

Hazel nodded and glanced into the swirling mist, certain she could see shapes stalking through it. 'It'll be easy for them to follow the wagon,' she said. 'They could attack us at any moment.'

'Correct,' Titus said. 'And we need to get help for David. The boy's a prize-winning fool, but he's *my* fool and I won't see him die. There are a few smallholdings in Wychwood . . . Forest people are strange and don't like outsiders, but they *might* help us. Though we won't get far in the wagon.'

'What if I take David into the forest while you draw them away in the wagon?'

Titus scowled. 'That'll do, I suppose. There's a bridge coming up that crosses a stream. Follow it east until you reach a cabin on a hill. It's not too far from here. But be careful – as I said, forest dwellers can be dangerous.'

'You said "strange" before.'

'I meant *dangerous*,' Titus said. 'You'll need to slip away unnoticed. There's a trapdoor under the rug inside. When we reach the bridge you and David can drop through on to the road and get away as fast as you can. If they're watching, they're less likely to notice if you leave that way. I'll draw those horrors off while you make your escape.'

'What about you?' asked Hazel. Although she was terrified of the Witch Finder, she didn't like leaving him at the mercy of Rawhead and Spindle.

'I can look after myself. And, girl?'

'Yes?'

'You are responsible for what happened to my fool. So see he gets help.'

With a nod she climbed through the hatch into the wagon. Samson wagged his tail and gave a little whine. David lay on the bottom bunk with his arm across his bandaged face, as if shielding himself from a bright light. His chest rose and fell in rapid gasps.

'David,' Hazel said, taking his hand. 'Wake up, we have to go.'

The flesh around the puncture wounds on his cheek was raw and moist. She flinched but didn't look away. 'What's wrong with me?' he rasped. 'Am I dying?'

'Not even slightly,' she said, forcing herself to smile.

'I don't remember what h-happened . . . just that vile spider and then . . . nothing.' His voice was paper-thin and creased with pain.

'We were ambushed. They're still after us, but there might be people nearby who can help. We need to get you out of here. Can you get up?'

David grimaced as he sat up. 'They've not killed me . . . yet.'

'Good.' Hazel grabbed her bag and pulled back the rug, revealing a trapdoor with a brass ring handle. She heaved it open. Cold air and threads of mist seeped inside.

David knelt beside her, face blanched with pain as he wound a bandage around his head to cover his wounded eye. The crunch of the wheels changed to a rumble as the wagon mounted the bridge.

'This is it.' Hazel said. 'Follow me as soon as I've jumped. Stay low – *they* may be watching.' She swung her legs over the edge. 'And Samson, be a good boy and stay here.' The dog whined but lay down by the stove.

'Here goes,' she said, and dropped through the hatch.

17

BACK IN THE FOREST

Witchcraft is a dark and horrible reality, an ever-present
menace, and a thing most active, perilous and true.
Der Hexenhammer by Dr Heinrich Hoefer

Hazel lay flat on her stomach as the wagon rumbled over her. David landed heavily a few feet away, grunting with pain.

'We need to get out of sight,' she hissed, watching the wagon disappear into the mist. She looked up as rain pattered against the leaves. Cool water fell on her face and she licked it from her lips. Its crisp taste sharpened her mind. 'Come on, let's get off the road,' she said, putting her arm around David's waist and helping him to his feet. They peered over the bridge parapet at steep banks studded with shrubs and mossy rocks. From the bottom, lost in shadow, rose the sound of rushing water. 'Ready?'

'No.' David heaved a rattling breath.

'Me neither. Let's go.'

She guided David off the bridge and over the edge of the bank. *How on earth did I end up in this situation?* she thought, stepping carefully on to what she hoped was a solid foothold. 'Step where I step, and take care –

it's slippery and a long way down.'

'Step where she steps, step where she steps, step where she steps . . .' David murmured.

'Oh dear,' said a small voice. Bramley had somehow scrabbled his way back up to his favourite perch behind her left ear. 'I think the poison is making him go doolally.'

It was raining hard by the time they were halfway down the embankment, soaked to the skin and gasping. Streams of water foamed down the slope, loosening the soil and stones. Desperate to get as far away from the road as possible, Hazel forced herself to descend slowly, helping David with every faltering step. Only the thought of him lying at the foot of the bank with a broken neck stopped her from going faster.

After an eternity of slips and near falls, they splashed into a puddle at the foot of the bank. The stream was swollen with floodwater, rushing in a torrent around jagged rocks.

'At least it drowns out our noise,' Bramley said, shivering. 'And perhaps covers our scent too.'

Movement on the bridge caught Hazel's eye and she pulled David behind a boulder. She put a finger to her lips. He nodded. Two silent figures crossed the bridge, one black, and one white, ghostlike in the miasmic rain. Hazel held her breath and only let it out after they had disappeared up the road.

'It worked,' she said. 'They're following the wagon.'

David staggered towards the riverbank. 'I c-can't leave him to face them alone,' he muttered. 'He's an old man . . .'

'Don't be stupid,' Hazel said, grabbing his arm. 'He told

me to get you to a safe place. Besides, you're in no state to fight. You'd just be a hindrance.' She sighed when his face fell. 'I'm sorry, but it's true.'

'All right,' he said, his teeth chattering. 'But first chance I get I'm going to k-kill that spider myself.'

Keeping to the shadows, Hazel and David followed the stream east, slipping on rocks and gasping as the freezing water gushed over their feet. Eventually they emerged from the cutting. The banks levelled out and the stream widened, flowing over a bed of flat, smooth stones.

Hazel looked up through a gap in the trees. The morning sky was drab: grey, dark and oppressive.

'I need to stop,' David croaked. 'Can we rest for a minute?'

'All right.' Hazel glanced at his haggard face. 'But not for too long.' She led him under the fronds of a willow tree and settled him down by its trunk. He sat for a moment with his head between his legs and then threw up on his boots.

'Oh, lovely,' Bramley said.

Hazel dipped the edge of her cloak in the river and wiped David's mouth and chin. *He's so pale*, she thought. *He looks dead already.* Guilt squirmed in her stomach.

'Step where she steps, step where she steps . . .' David mumbled.

Hazel sat next to him and snuggled deeper into her cloak. 'David,' she said – realizing the boy had fallen silent. '*David?*'

He stirred and opened his good eye. 'Oh. So it wasn't a bad dream.'

'I'm afraid not,' she said with a small smile.

'Those people back there, they might still be after us. You . . . you should go on without me. I'm only slowing you down . . .' His eye flickered and his head lolled on to his chest.

I could leave him, she thought. *After all, he'd probably kill me if he knew I was a witch.* She shook her head violently to dispel such dark thoughts – dislodging Bramley in the process. He gave an indignant squeak.

'Don't be such a blockhead,' she said, giving David a shake. 'We're sticking together. I'm paying you to find my ma, remember, and I don't pay the dead. Now come on, we can't stay here all day.'

David groaned as she helped him to his feet. 'You're as s-stubborn as the boss.'

'And don't you forget it.' She jumped as a flash lit up the clouds, followed by a sound like a splitting tree trunk.

'That sounded like the c-cannon,' David wheezed. 'The b-boss is in trouble.'

'I'm sure he can look after himself,' Hazel replied, trying to sound confident.

'I hope so.' David took a ragged gasp. 'For all our sakes.'

18

THE CABIN IN THE WOODS

'I know the danger Wielders could pose if driven
underground. I deem it wise to grant them
protection – that way I can control them.'
Charles Stuart, King of England, Scotland and Ireland, 1634

Hazel couldn't tell what time it was when they eventually emerged from the forest into a clearing. Did the sunless gloom signify noon or dusk? Bramley had fallen asleep in her cloak pocket some time ago and David could barely walk, let alone make conversation.

Hope welled up in her when she looked up the grassy slope and saw a cabin surrounded by a kitchen garden.

A cabin on a hill. This must be the place Titus talked about.

A path lined with beanpoles wound its way between vegetable patches full of spinach, cabbages and cauliflowers. The air smelt of wild garlic and the onions that grew in abundant clumps.

Hazel hefted David more securely under her arm. 'Look, we've found somewhere to shelter.'

'Thank g-goodness,' he said. 'I don't think I c-can go on for m-much longer.'

They made their way up the path, Hazel willing her

116

wobbling legs to cover the last few yards. The smell of herbs was so like that at home it made her heart ache. The cabin overlooked the garden from under the sheltering arms of an oak tree. Ivy trailed from over the front door to the roof of a little outhouse built a few feet from the sidewall.

Hazel halted on the threshold. Disappointment swallowed her relief in one gulp. The cabin door swung on its hinges, no smoke rose from the chimney and the windows were dark.

'Hello? Is anyone home?' she called, pushing open the door and helping David inside. There was no answer.

The kitchen had a sink, an open fireplace and shelves crammed with glass jars and bottles. A saucepan and two cups sat on the table. Feeble light struggled through the windows and down a narrow staircase leading to an attic room.

What a lonely place to live, Hazel thought. *But with a fire it could be cosy.*

'Deserted,' David croaked as he lowered himself into a chair by the table.

'It seems so. But someone was here not long ago, so they'll probably be back soon. At least we can rest in the dry for a while.' Hazel found a tinderbox and lit a candle. She held it up to David's face and gently lifted the bandage from his eye. Somehow she managed not to flinch from what she saw.

'W-well?' he said through chattering teeth. 'How do I l-look?'

117

'Well, the swelling's gone down a bit.' She didn't mention how the puncture wounds in his neck and cheek were festering and going green. 'How do you feel?'

'Sick. My eye burns. Can't seem . . . to catch my breath.'

'Let's get you to bed. Come on.' Hazel hoisted him to his feet.

'I'm so cold.' David said, leaning heavily on Hazel. 'Cold as death.'

It took several exhausting minutes to get up the stairs, where they found a bedroom with an unmade truckle bed, a wardrobe and a fireplace full of ash. The floor was strewn with rushes. Hazel set the candle down on the bedside table and lowered David on to the mattress. He twitched and moaned and drew in rattling breaths.

'Here we are,' she said, trying to sound cheerful. 'I'll just take off your coat and boots – then I can tuck you in.'

'I'm n-not a child.'

'Sorry,' Hazel said. As she pulled off his boot, a pocket-sized pistol and a pouch of shot and gunpowder fell to the floor. She gingerly picked them up and put them on the bedside table.

In the corner of the room was a jug of water and a bowl. The water looked fairly fresh so she soaked a cloth and began to wipe David's brow.

'Am I going to d-die here?' he said. 'So far from home?'

'No, you're not.' Hazel squeezed out the cloth and dipped it back into the bowl. 'Titus will come back for us, I know it.'

118

'He's d-dead already. The spider will g-get him.' David lurched up, scrabbling at his throat. 'I can feel its fangs,' he cried. 'Get them out!'

'Hush,' Hazel said, pushing him back on to the pillows. 'It's gone. You're safe here. I'm going to look after you.'

David thrashed left and right, staring at something past her shoulder.

'David, look at me,' she said, struggling to hold him still. 'Tell me about Titus. Where did you meet him?'

David went limp and Hazel felt some of his strength ebb away. 'I d-didn't meet him, I *found* him.' He paused to catch his breath. 'Drunk and p-penniless in a tavern in Cirencester. A great d-disappointment to me.'

Hazel let go of his shoulders. 'Why's that?'

'I grew up hearing tales about the g-great Titus White. I wanted to be a Witch Finder more than anything – all because of him.'

'So Titus was famous?'

He frowned at her. 'You've r-really never heard of him?' His breath gurgled in his chest. 'As s-soon as I came of age, and against my father's wishes, I left home to find the great Titus White and convince him to t-take me on as his apprentice. It took me nearly a year to track him down.'

The more David talked the calmer he became, so Hazel probed further. 'Why was he so hard to find? What happened to him?'

'I don't know. Before the w-war he was feted, celebrated, *famous*. But afterwards, all I know – all *anyone* knows – is that he d-disappeared into a wine bottle and never came out.'

'What happened when you found him?' Hazel asked.

'I managed to cajole him into swearing me in as his apprentice. I hoped going b-back on the road as a Witch Finder would give him a new lease of life. I wanted to learn from him, from the b-best. But without a Witch Hunter's licence we couldn't get much work, and Titus drank away what little we earned.' He sighed. 'Look where all my grand plans have g-got me. A poor end for the son of a d-duke, don't you think?'

'You're not going to die,' Hazel said, taking his hand and squeezing. 'I won't let you.'

'Everyone dies,' David muttered. 'You, me . . . everyone.' His eye fluttered closed and he fell asleep.

Hazel pulled the blanket up to his neck, staring at his white face and the rotten flesh around the bandage.

'I need to treat his wounds,' she muttered as she hurried downstairs.

'What's going on?' yawned Bramley, crawling out from her hair.

'Oh, you've decided to wake up, have you?'

'We mice need a lot of sleep,' he said. 'How's the boy?'

'Sick. Very sick. A poultice of some kind might help to draw out the poison. I'll need a piece of cloth, er . . . some bran and some linseed . . . ?' She squeezed her eyes shut in frustration. 'If only I'd paid more attention when Ma was going on about medicines.'

'There's no point moaning,' Bramley said. 'You'll have to make do with what you know.'

A frantic search of the cupboards and shelves failed to produce the ingredients Hazel needed. 'There's nothing here,' she said, sitting down. 'David's dying and I can't help him.' She slammed her fist on to the table, rattling the cups.

Bramley scampered down her arm and pointed a tiny claw at her. 'Now listen – we're not beaten yet. That boy needs help, not tears, so buck up and think of a plan.'

Hazel took a shaky breath. 'You're right, Bram. I'm just so tired of being afraid all the time.'

'We just need to hang on until the old man finds us,' Bramley said. 'Seems odd to be telling a witch that everything is going to be all right when the Witch Finder turns up . . .'

Hazel groaned.

'Now, what's the plan?'

'I'll take a look in that outhouse. Who knows?' she said, brightening a little. 'It might be filled to bursting with medicine, pies and apples.' She shrugged off her wet cloak and draped it over a chair. 'You wait here. Come and fetch me if David calls out.'

'I'll guard the cabin until you get back,' Bramley said, puffing out his chest. 'But don't be long.'

'I won't. And don't fall asleep.'

'As if I'd do such a thing!'

Hazel opened the crooked outhouse door and poked her head into a windowless room stacked with barrels and bulging sacks of vegetables. A brace of rabbits hung head down from the ceiling, black eyes staring.

I'm glad I left Bram behind, she thought, filling a basket with some vegetables and a small bag of bran for the poultice. *I wouldn't want him to see them.*

She was about to leave when she saw a doll made of straw hanging from a nail in the wall. Its head was covered with a piece of cloth tied around the neck.

That'll do as kindling, Hazel thought as she unhooked it and put it in her basket.

In the darkness of the storeroom, she didn't notice the twisted symbols scored on the inside of the door, or the doll twitch like a living thing the moment she crossed the threshold.

19

THE POPPET

*When prosecuting a witch, Witch Hunters are encouraged
to use fear and intimidation to extract information.*
Amendment to the Witch Laws, 1653

By the time Hazel returned to the kitchen with her ingredients, Bramley had curled up in a teacup and fallen asleep again.

I knew it! she thought. *Lazy little fur-ball.*

Leaving him to his mousy dreams, she set to work making up the poultice and chopping vegetables. The smell of the onions and garlic made her realize how hungry she was.

I'll cook the soup in the bedroom, she thought, picking up the pan and climbing the stairs. *The smell of food might revive David.*

When she entered the bedroom David was moaning in his sleep and gripping the blanket with white-knuckled fists. Hazel knelt by the fireplace, sick with a feeling of guilt and responsibility. She laid the doll on the ash pile, placed a few logs around it and was about to strike the tinderbox when something made her stop. She stared at the doll, with its outstretched arms and blank face.

What a strange thing you are, she thought, pulling it

123

out and tucking it into her belt. *It feels wrong to burn you. Besides, I'm a Fire Witch – I don't need kindling.*

After checking to ensure that David was still asleep, she concentrated on the magic flickering like a lantern inside her. *I have to learn how to cast my magic properly, to control it.*

She closed her eyes, concentrating hard to draw a tiny quantity of magic from her heart, and pushed the tickling warmth down her arms. Tongues of flame licked the skin on the back of her hands, and with a deft flick she sent a sizzling burst of magic into the grate. A delighted yelp of laughter escaped her as flames caught under the logs. They crackled and snapped, warming her face.

I did it, she thought, rubbing her tingling fingers together. *I'm learning how to control it.* Enjoying the heat – *her* heat! – she hung the pan over the fire.

'What did you just do? How did you m-make that fire?'

Hazel's heart crawled into her throat. It was David's voice. She turned round, cursing herself for her recklessness. David was sitting bolt upright in bed, his uncovered eye staring at her wildly.

'I just used wood shavings and oil,' she said, forcing a smile. 'It went up so quickly it nearly took off my eyebrows.'

'I saw fire coming out of your fingers . . . Hazel, what's going on?'

'Nothing,' Hazel said, her heart hammering. 'I'm just making you some food—'

'I saw you . . .' The confusion on his face crumpled into

124

fear and before Hazel could move he grabbed the pistol from the bedside table and aimed it at her. 'Stay back!'

'David,' she said, holding out her hands. 'Please, put that down.'

'You lied to me.' His eye narrowed. 'You're n-not one of us at all.'

'Don't be silly—'

'You're a w-witch. A *Wielder*.' He spat the word out like poison.

Hazel took a hesitant step forward. 'You're sick, delirious. David, you can barely see.'

His face flickered with uncertainty, but the pistol didn't waver. She stared down the barrel, expecting it to explode at any moment.

'What's that?' he said, pointing to the straw doll in her belt. 'Is that yours?'

'What, this? I found it in the outhouse. I was going to use it as kindling.'

'Show me,' David said.

Hazel tossed the doll on to the bed and David picked it up with shaking fingers. 'Tell me what you need this for. Quickly!'

'I don't need it for anything,' she said. 'I've never seen such a curious thing before. It's not mine, I swear.'

'Don't play innocent with me. This is a poppet, a witch's tool of sorcery. What were you g-going to do with it? Lay a curse on m-me? Kill me?'

Everything was spinning out of control and Hazel didn't

know what to do. 'Think about what you're saying. Why would I have carried you here if all I wanted to do was kill you?'

He fell back on to the bed, shaking with exhaustion. 'You lied to me. And I fell for it.'

'No, I promise I didn't lie. The demon's poison is making your mind play tricks on you.' She crept forward and took the pistol from him. 'David, I'm your friend. I don't want to hurt you.'

'Tell me again,' the boy wheezed, refusing to look at her. 'Where d-did you find it?'

'In the outhouse.'

'Didn't you think it would be b-best to just leave it alone?'

'I didn't know—'

'You should have left it there.' His teeth chattered despite the warmth of the fire. 'The boss once told me about a witch who murdered a merchant. She strangled h-him with a horse whip and used b-black magic to rip out his soul and trap it in a straw doll.'

Cold fingers traced down Hazel's spine as she waited for David to continue.

'But that was not the worst of it – b-because as the soul found no rest, n-neither could the corpse, so it wandered the moors, searching for a p-peace it would never find.'

Hazel picked up the poppet and held it gingerly in front of her. Outside, the wind whispered around the eaves.

'How do you know that this doll was used for the same thing?' she asked.

'The boss said the witch's doll had its head w-wrapped in cloth, just like th-that one. It could be calling out right now.'

'Calling out?' asked Hazel. 'To what?'

'Its mortal remains.'

20

MORTAL REMAINS

Fear will not hold me back.
I am ready to face the Lord of Flies.

Extract from the diary of Grand Magus Lars Göran Petrov

Hazel tried to wrap her mind around what David had just said. 'Are you trying to tell me that if there is a soul trapped in this doll, it is going to start calling out to . . . *its dead body?*'

He opened his eye and nodded.

'But . . . whose?'

'How the h-hell should I know? That poppet c-could have been here for years until you d-disturbed it.'

'I hate to say this,' Hazel took a deep breath, 'but this looks new to me. The straw's fresh.'

She hugged herself and looked through the grimy window at the shadowed skirts of the forest. Something caught her eye. Movement. She dragged her gaze towards it, quaking with dread.

A *thing* edged up the garden path; a wasted husk of human remains wrapped in rags, crawling on its stomach like a wounded animal. A canvas sack, tied to a choke around the neck, covered its head.

Hazel wiped a trembling hand over the misty window and shut her eyes. *It's not real. When I open my eyes it'll be gone. Please, please be gone.* She opened her eyes; it was still there, and closer. Closer to the door. The *unlocked* door.

'Something's out there,' she croaked. 'It's standing up . . . it's *pointing* at me.'

The little colour left in David's face drained away. 'Put the poppet back where you found it. It's our only—' he collapsed back, his good eye rolling up into his head.

The thing, whatever it was, lurched up the path. Clods of mud stuck to its rags. *Like it's crawled from the ground,* thought Hazel. *From its grave . . .*

She grabbed the poppet, dashed down the stairs and stopped dead by the door. She swayed on her heels, staring at the solid wood and stout latch. In her mind's eye she saw the creature waiting for her on the other side – arms outstretched and ready to grab her.

How far is it to the outhouse? She desperately tried to recall how many steps it was. *Will I get there before it catches me?*

Her hand closed over the handle and she threw open the door.

The thing crouched on the threshold, close enough for her to see its cracked fingernails reaching for her. Rot enveloped it like an invisible shroud. Paralysed with terror, Hazel could only stare.

'For pity's sake, close the door,' Bramley squeaked, standing up in his teacup.

Hazel slammed the door and slid home the bolt. A second later the creature crashed into it. The planks shivered under the blow and the wood around the hinges cracked. Hazel backed away.

'Pick me up, *pick me up*,' Bramley cried. Hazel lifted him from the cup and placed him on her shoulder. 'What was . . . *that?*'

'I don't know.' Still staring at the rattling door, Hazel retrieved the poppet from the floor. 'Whatever it is, I think it wants this.'

'Then give it back!'

Hazel dashed to the windows to check they were closed, and then heaved the heavy kitchen table in front of the door. 'I'm not letting that *thing* in here. We'll just have to hold on until Titus finds us.'

'And what if he doesn't?'

Hazel had no answer. She climbed the stairs, closed the bedroom door and jammed a chair under the handle. Feeling her heart slow a little, she perched on the bed next to the unconscious David, worrying the hem of her dress with trembling fingers. The crashing from downstairs finally stopped. Everything went quiet.

'Do you think—?'

A low moan came from outside; there were no words, but the desolation in the sound chilled Hazel to her bones.

'It's circling the cottage,' she whispered. 'Trying to find a way in.'

Branches scraped against a downstairs window. Hazel

put her hands over her ears to shut it out. 'It can't get in, it can't get in . . .'

Leaves rustled on the far side of the cabin, and then slowly the moaning faded away. Hazel waited. The silence stretched, disturbed only by David's laboured breathing.

'Has it gone?' Bramley said.

'I think so. For now, at least.'

Hazel stood up and put him on the windowsill. Together, they peered out of the window at the empty garden. Clouds sagged, scraping the treetops as if weary of holding so much rain. She turned away and looked at David.

'He knows, Bram,' she said. 'He knows I'm a witch.'

'What?' Bramley spluttered. 'How did he find out?'

'He saw me use magic to light the fire.'

Bramley slapped a paw to his forehead. 'You couldn't have kept it secret for just a few days?'

'It was so cold, and David was freezing . . . I was trying to do the right thing.'

'You haven't done the right thing since we left the Glade,' Bramley snapped.

They fell into a sullen silence. Hazel moved to the fire and stared into the flames.

'Are you going to leave me up here forever?' Bramley said from the windowsill.

'Yes,' Hazel said.

The fire crackled, sending sparks up the chimney.

'You do know that the first thing the boy will do when Titus gets back is tell him you're a witch,' Bramley said.

131

'Of course I know that.' Hazel slumped to the floor.

'So? Don't you think it'd be best not to be here when he does?'

'You mean we should just leave him?'

'I know you liked the boy,' Bramley said. 'But he's our enemy now.'

Beneath the bandages across David's face, Hazel saw the once handsome boy who had agreed to help her find her mother. She shook her head. 'I can't leave him. It's my fault he's here in the first place. It's my fault he might die.'

'But—'

'Enough.' Hazel got up and tapped Bramley on his twitching nose. 'Not another word.' She picked him up and tucked him behind her ear. 'I mean, look on the bright side – if that creature comes back, we'll be dead long before Titus gets a chance to kill us.'

21

A GLINT OF SILVER

*In England, Witch Hunters are regarded with
a mixture of respect and terror. In France they
are celebrated for being wildly heroic.*
Travels with a French Witch Hunter by Markus Corrigan

Alone on a frozen lake, the shores lost in mist. Her bare feet crunch on frost. Above, a starless sky stares down coldly. Below, black water swirls under ice. As she walks, a spider's web of cracks begins to radiate around her . . .

Hazel awoke with a start, the cracking of the ice becoming the crackle of the fire. It took a few moments to remember where she was. Dusk settled under a dark blue sky studded with stars. David was still asleep, his face tight with fatigue.

'Bram,' she whispered as she stoked some life into the fire. 'Are you awake?'

'No,' he grumbled from his nest in her hair.

She got up and sat in the chair next to the bed. David stirred, his one healthy eye roving under the lid. The simmering stew on the hearth didn't mask the ripe smell coming from his wounds. 'I'll have to change his dressings when he wakes up,' she said, wondering where she might find more bandages.

Bramley crawled out of her hair and perched on her

shoulder. 'I was having such a nice dream. I was back in my nest in the Glade and it was the beginning of summer.' He sighed. 'My favourite season.'

'I always liked autumn best – the colour of the leaves and the smell of woodsmoke.' Hazel pulled the blanket back over David's shoulders. 'Ma used to have nightmares sometimes. She used to wake up screaming.'

Bramley pressed his warm body against her neck. 'What were they about?'

'She'd never tell me, no matter how many times I asked. They were always more frequent during winter when the frosts were bad.' Hazel clasped her hands in her lap and stared into the fire. 'It used to scare me when she woke up crying in the dead of night. But I'd lie next to her and stroke her hair until she went back to sleep, wondering what could have happened to make her have such terrible dreams.' She sighed. 'After what we've been through these past few days, I think I'm beginning to understand.'

Bramley nudged her ear with his whiskery nose.

'Next morning, she'd get up and we'd talk about the harvest and the garden, and the latest mischief old Tom had got into – never about the nightmares.' A sense of loss crushed down on her. 'I just want her back, safe and sound where she belongs. With me.'

'We'll find her,' Bramley said. 'You'll see.'

They sat for a while, bathed in the glow of the fire as night cast its cloak over the outside world. Hazel was just dropping into a doze when she heard a hollow moan, seeping out of the forest and getting closer.

'It's come back,' she whispered. The ivy trailing up the outer wall rustled. 'It's trying to climb up.'

'Why?' Bramley squeaked. 'It can't get in through the bedroom windows – they're too small.'

Hazel looked up at the ceiling, at the widely spaced beams and the layer of thatch resting on top. 'It's going for the roof. That's its way in.'

Bramley buried his face in his paws. 'Why us? Why *me*?'

Hazel could tell from the rustling that it was already level with the bedroom and climbing higher. The rustling stopped just below the eaves.

'Maybe it's—'

There was a thump and then a fevered scrabbling over their heads. The thatch sagged. It was on the roof.

Hazel shook David roughly by the shoulder and screamed in his face. 'Wake up! Oh, you stupid boy, wake *up*, will you?'

'Leave him,' Bramley said. 'You can't help him now. Let's go before that thing gets in. Who knows what it'll do to us?'

'I *won't* leave him.' Hazel followed the rustling of straw as the thing crawled away from the edge of the roof. It stopped over the bed. David's pistol lay on the windowsill, but she didn't know how it worked, or even if it was loaded.

'What are you going to do then? Ask it nicely to leave? Oh *I* see,' he said as Hazel wrapped her hands in her skirt and unhooked the steaming pan from over the fire. 'You're going to feed it to death.'

'Quiet, mouse.' Hazel backed into a corner, watching the bulge in the ceiling. Strands of straw drifted down on to the bed. 'I'm going to fight it.'

'With soup?'

She glanced at David. If he woke up now they might have a chance to get out of the cabin and escape. *And then what? No*, she said to herself. *I've got to end this here.* The pan was heavy and her arms started to shake. Lumpy stew spilt on to the floor.

The scratching stopped.

Hazel pressed her back against the wall as an arm burst into the room. Bones clicked as it ripped away a handful of thatch, revealing a patch of night sky.

Hazel gripped the pan tightly as the creature's furious assault on the thatch forced a hole big enough for it to push its head and shoulders into the room. It hung upside down like an enormous bat, twisting round to face her.

'How can it see us through the sack?' Bramley yelped.

The corpse crashed to the foot of the bed in a shower of debris. Clambering jerkily to its feet, it reached out with mould-streaked arms.

Hazel hurled the pan as hard as she could. It flew through the air, spraying brown lumps of stew in every direction and bashing the creature on its head. Knocked off its feet, it collided with the chair jammed under the door and smashed it to pieces. Drenched in stew, it lay whimpering in the wreckage.

Shaking all over, Hazel picked up the pan and brandished it like a weapon. The firelight glinted on something around the thing's wrist. *I recognize that bracelet . . .*

'Oh no,' she cried, dropping the pan. *'Mary.'*

22
BLIND MARY APPLEGATE

'This is your friend, *Blind Mary*?' Bramley gasped from his hiding place in her curls. 'What happened to her?'

'I don't know,' Hazel said, her voice heavy with grief. 'I should have recognized her earlier.' She knelt down and helped her old friend sit up against the wall. 'Mary, it's me, Hazel. Can you hear me?'

Mary nodded, moaning quietly.

'Mary, dear,' Hazel said, reaching out, 'I'm going to untie your head so I can see you.' Mary wailed and grabbed the sack with both hands. 'All right, we'll leave that on for now. Can you stand up? Here, take my hand.' Mary's fingers felt as fragile as bird bones. 'Up you get.'

'Give her back the poppet,' Bramley said. 'Perhaps that'll make her feel better.'

Hazel held it out. 'Here you are. Take it if you want.'

Mary drew it to her breast and let out a long sigh.

'Get away from her,' shrieked a voice from behind them. It was David, shivering with fever, drenched in sweat and aiming his pistol straight at Mary.

'David, no! It's all right, she's—' Hazel began, but before she could move, he pulled the trigger.

The pistol roared, filling the room with smoke. The shot buzzed passed Hazel's ear, causing her to step back and slip on spilt potage. There was a *whump* and a hole appeared in Mary's chest. Shreds of fabric blew out in a powdery cloud. Knocked clean off her feet, the old witch fell backwards through the flimsy wooden door and down the stairs.

Hazel grabbed the bedpost, aware of a high-pitched whine in her left ear. David fumbled as he tried to reload his pistol.

'Quick, close the door,' he said, 'before that . . . *thing* . . . c-comes back.'

'You stupid boy,' Hazel gasped. 'She wasn't going to hurt us.'

David goggled at her. 'What are you—? It's a dead thing, an abomination—'

'She's my friend,' Hazel bristled at him. 'And I'm going downstairs to help her.'

'Your friend?' David's face hardened. 'A witch, I suppose – just like you. I'm really at your mercy now, aren't I?'

Hazel grabbed the pistol from him. 'Don't be so soft-brained. No harm's coming to you. Just trust me.'

'Never t-trust a witch,' David said.

Hazel tucked the pistol into her belt, covered David with the blankets and left the room. She found Mary in the kitchen, clutching the poppet to her chest. Smoke drifted

139

from the hole in her chest but there was no blood.

'Mary,' Hazel said. 'Can you speak?'

Mary shook her head, She shuffled to the dresser and took out a roll of parchment, a bottle of ink and a peacock-feather quill with a silver nib. Beckoning for Hazel to join her at the kitchen table, she sat down and flattened out the parchment.

Hazel sat opposite, tears prickling behind her eyes. Somewhere under the dirt-caked clothes was Mary, her old friend. A knot of anger hardened inside her. *I know who did this*, she thought. *And I'll get him for it, too.*

Mary dipped the quill into the ink and began to write.

Dearest Hazel, It shames me for you to see me so rotten and faded.

'Oh, Mary,' Hazel said, tears falling freely now. 'You mustn't feel ashamed – this isn't your fault. Can you tell me what happened? What can I do to help?'

First I must ask – where is your mother?

Hazel looked down at the table and told Mary everything; after she had finished, Mary put her head in her hands and moaned.

'It's all right,' Hazel said. 'I'm going to find Ma and bring her home. You can come and live with us and we'll look after you, I promise.'

Mary picked up the quill and started scribbling.

This is all my fault. I told Murrell where you lived, and how to get through the Border Hedge.

'So it *was* him who did this to you.'

He told me he'd feed me to his demon if I didn't do what he asked and I was too weak to stand up to him. He wanted your mother and her healing magic, and I gave her up. But I didn't tell him about you, little Hazel. I kept you a secret, because I knew he'd want you too.

'Well, he knows all about me now,' Hazel said with a small smile.

I'm so sorry.

Hazel thought of Mary, all alone, being menaced by Murrell and Rawhead. 'This isn't your fault. Can you tell me what happened?'

After I told him where to find Hecate, he said he wanted my help to fight the Witch Hunters. I refused. The scratching quill flew across the parchment. *He said I deserved to be punished for betraying the cause, so he*

The quill stopped. A blob of ink formed around the nib. Hazel waited, chewing on a strand of hair.

sentenced me to this death state. He trapped my soul in this doll – she caressed the ugly thing as if it was a beloved child – *then buried my body in the garden to rot. I felt every shovelful of cold earth fall on me. Then darkness, silence.*

Mary stopped writing.

'I found the doll in the outhouse,' Hazel said with a growing sense of horror. 'I was going to burn it . . .'

When you removed the poppet from the magic

141

circle it cried out. My body heard, and dug its way out of the grave. Her head drooped. *Body and soul together, but still apart.*

'Is there anything I can do to help?'

No. My body is crumbling. I'm so tired. I just want to sleep forever.

'There must be something I can do,' Hazel said miserably.

You must listen - I have something to tell you.

'What?'

Your mother - I think I know where she is.

Hazel's eyes widened. 'You do?'

Murrell told me he and his followers are planning to gather at Rivenpike. It's a town not far from here.

'Then that's where I must go.'

Be careful. He took your mother because he wants to use her magic, although I don't know why. Murrell will want you too now that he knows you can wield fire. Don't get drawn into his war - it'll be the death of you.

'I understand. Thank you, Mary.' She looked up the stairs. *I wonder if David's been listening.* 'Mary, will you do one more thing for me?'

Anything.

'The boy I'm travelling with has been poisoned. Can you help him?'

I can try. Mary put down the pen.

A few hours later Hazel closed the cabin door, dropped the shovel on the kitchen floor and slumped down in the rocking chair. She stared numbly at her muddy, blistered hands. Mary's final note lay on the table.

The boy will live, but he's half blind and will be in pain for a long time – demon wounds never fully heal. I think I drew out most of the poison, but there may be some left and I don't know how it will affect him.

Her final words were a jagged scrawl:

I am tired of this cold world. Bury me next to Gander. I might find peace there.

Bramley stroked Hazel's neck with his cheek, absorbing her sorrow until she fell asleep.

23

SECRETS AND LIES

*'For a pure conscience, I'll do no wrong. For a pure soul,
I'll pray every day. For a pure England, I'll burn every witch.'*
Lord Protector Oliver Cromwell

Hazel awoke to the sound of someone pouring water into a cup. She felt a thin, straw mattress underneath her and a blanket pulled up to her neck. The smell of woodsmoke and leather told her that she was back in the wagon.

So, she thought, her relief giving way to trepidation, *Titus has found us, and I bet David's told him about me being a witch. Oh, Bram, we're really in trouble now.*

Where *was* Bramley? She couldn't feel him nesting in her hair or fidgeting in her pocket. He was gone. Panic ripped through her, and her first instinct was to leap up and look for him, to scream his name, but she stayed still.

'Ah,' Titus said. 'You're awake.'

Hazel's heart fluttered, but she kept her eyes closed.

'See, David, how her breathing sped up and her eyes started moving under the lids? That's how I know she's only pretending to sleep and she's actually listening to every word I'm saying.'

Realizing she had no choice, Hazel opened her eyes and

144

saw Titus watching her from a chair next to the bed, shirt sleeves rolled up over strong arms. A cloud of smoke drifted from his pipe.

David sat at the workbench, glaring over his shoulder at her. A clean bandage covered his left eye; the skin around the edge was blotchy. Samson lay by the stove, chewing on a bone.

'Morning, slop-sprite,' Titus said, holding out a cup. Hazel pushed herself up on her elbows and took it. 'Seems we all made it through our travails to be reunited again.'

David snorted and went back to filling cartridges with gunpowder. Hazel took a sip of water and decided it was best to keep quiet until she had a better idea of what the old Witch Finder knew, and more importantly, what he intended to do about it.

'Aren't you going to ask me how I fared against our ambushers?' he said.

Hazel nodded, keeping her face calm despite the panic breaking out just beneath the surface. *Bram, you silly mouse, where are you?*

'Well, our ruse worked,' Titus continued. 'Our ambushers didn't see you escape so they followed me in the wagon. I gave them a bloody nose for their trouble, and they lost interest when they realized you weren't with me. And here I am, good as my word.'

'I'm glad to see you safe,' Hazel said.

'You seem ill at ease.'

Act normally. Just act normally.

145

She rolled her eyes. 'Of course I am. Who wouldn't be after what just happened?'

Titus took a pull on his pipe. 'David's been through the wringer too, of course. He told me what happened in the cabin.'

Hazel saw David's shoulders stiffen. 'Oh?' she said, waiting for the accusation.

'He says you used magic,' Titus said. 'Saw you create fire –' Hazel flinched when he snapped his fingers – 'from thin air.'

'Yes,' she said, keeping her voice calm. 'Poor David was raving about it when his fever was at its worst. I'd just lit the fire to keep him warm when he started shouting all sorts of nonsense at me. I thought he'd gone mad.'

Titus shook his head. 'As I thought,' he sighed.

Does he believe me, or David? Hazel wished she could read his expression.

'I told him that Wielders who control the elements are very rare,' Titus continued. 'Especially now. Most died in the Witch War, and the rest are being hunted to extinction by Cromwell and his Witch Hunters.'

Hazel didn't move as Titus refilled her cup. Slowly, slowly, she forced herself to relax.

'I know what I saw,' David muttered.

Titus waved his hand. 'Maybe. Maybe not. That spider's poison was eating at your wits as well as your eye. And let's not forget, this girl saved your life.' He tapped his pipe out into a bowl and refilled it from the tobacco jar.

Hazel sized Titus up from over the rim of her cup. He looked sober. His eyes were bright and he'd even combed his beard and hair. This was not the addled wreck she'd encountered in Watley gaol. This, perhaps, was the legendary Witch Finder David had told her about.

'That man in the forest who attacked us, do you know anything about him?' Titus asked.

Hazel shook her head. 'Only that it was his demon who kidnapped my ma.'

'And why would he do such a thing, I wonder?' He took a match from his pocket and struck it on the table. A yellow flame flared.

'I've already told you. I don't know. But he said he knew you. Is that true?'

Titus watched her through a fresh cloud of pipe smoke. 'Yes, I believe it is. I'm pretty sure he is one Nicolas Murrell. I recognized his voice from under the hood, although I sense he has changed much since I last saw him.' He took a long pull on his pipe, lost in thought. 'But then, I've changed too, have I not, David?'

Apprentice glanced at master, face unreadable.

'Were you hunting him?' Hazel asked.

'That's a story for another time,' Titus replied. 'Suffice to say that Murrell is obsessed with demonic magic – he's studied that forbidden art for years. I knew him before the war when he worked for the King. The last I heard he'd been captured by Cromwell, but it seems he's escaped.'

147

'But what would a man like that want with me?' Hazel said. *Or Ma?*

'That, slop-sprite, is a very good question.'

Doesn't he ever blink? she thought, struggling to hold his gaze. *If I look away, he'll think I'm acting guiltily.* The wagon felt uncomfortably hot. A drop of sweat ran down her neck.

'Well?' he continued. 'What would an outlawed demon-worshipper want with you and your mother?'

Ma always told me that guilty people parry when they're accused, Hazel thought. *But innocent people get angry . . .*

'For the last time, *I don't know,*' she snapped. 'That's what I employed you and David to find out. So far I don't feel like I'm getting my money's worth. Ma's *still* missing and you're wasting time asking me stupid questions you *know* I can't answer.'

'Questions are my stock-in-trade, slop-sprite. What about Mary? David said you knew her.'

Hazel's mind whirled. Should she lie about this too? Being connected to a witch like Mary would cast more suspicion on her, yet instinct told her that trying to deceive Titus about it would be a mistake.

'Mary? Yes, I know – *knew* – her.'

'I thought so. The care with which you buried her and the flowers on the grave confirms that. How did you come to meet her?'

Hazel took a sip of water, biding her time. She set her cup down on the floor and clasped her hands in her lap.

'Ma and I knew her only in passing. She was eccentric, but harmless enough.'

A smile flickered across Titus's face. 'Eccentric she may have been, but she was far from harmless. Would it surprise you if I told you that I knew old Mary too?'

'I don't know anything about Mary's friends.' Hazel shrugged, wondering if this was a ploy to trip her up.

'I met her during the course of my duties. You see, Mary was a witch.'

'A witch?' Hazel said, widening her eyes in feigned surprise. 'I had no idea.'

David leaped from his seat. 'She's lying. She said this Mary was her friend, and I *did* see her conjure fire. Why do you believe her and not me?'

'Sit down, boy,' Titus growled.

'Well, don't blame me if she kills us both as soon as our backs are turned,' David muttered.

Titus leaned back in his chair and stretched out his legs. 'I oversaw a case where Mary was accused of witchcraft. This was long before the Witch War, and I was still a young man – beardless, in fact.'

Hazel sat up, and even David swivelled in his chair to listen.

'A local farmer called Fawcett had accused Mary of laying a curse on his cattle. He claimed he'd seen her smearing blood on their haunches and chanting at the moon, and two days later all his cows were dying of the black flux.'

He paused to relight his pipe. 'Now, this was my first

case as a Witch Finder, and I decided to speak to Fawcett first. On the way to his farm I found the dead cows in his pasture, covered in flies and bloating in the sun. Each beast had had a tooth ripped from its mouth – part of a black magic ritual.

'Fawcett was surprised to see me, nervous too – said he'd expected me to have already arrested Mary on his word alone.' Titus shook his head. 'But men lie, and I wanted the truth.'

Hazel watched as Titus stared deep into a distant memory.

'So I took him to Watley gaol and left him in a cell to stew, taking care to leave my bag in there with him.' He smiled grimly. 'I watched him through the keyhole. He sweated and shook and couldn't take his eyes off that bag. "What instruments of torture are in there?" he was thinking. "Thumbscrews? Teeth-pullers? A choke pear? Heretic's fork?" I waited as he drove himself half mad imagining all the awful things I was going to do to him. And what do you think happened when I opened the door?'

Hazel shook her head and was surprised to see a wide smile spread across the Witch Finder's face, crinkling his eyes and making the years fall away.

'Peed himself,' he said with a laugh. 'Then he confessed to lying about Mary. He even admitted that he and his wife had pulled the cows' teeth out to make it look like black magic. Case closed, and all without having to ask a single question.'

'And what *was* in your bag?' Hazel asked.

'My lunch. Ham, cheese, an apple. Certainly no torture devices. I never have and never would use such things.'

He's lying, Hazel thought. *Trying to get me to trust him.*

'What about Mary?' she said, watching for any flicker of untruth in the old man's eyes.

'I went to see her, just to satisfy my own curiosity. It was obvious that although she had a touch of magic about her, she was not an evildoer. So I left her alone.'

'But why did Fawcett accuse her? What did he hope to gain?' David asked.

'Fawcett was dirt poor with a family to feed. When his cows got sick he became desperate, so he and his wife devised a plan. In those days, if livestock fell ill due to witchcraft the farmer would receive compensation from the King. But if they got sick through natural causes they'd get nothing.'

'So he accused Mary to claim the King's compensation?' Hazel said.

Titus nodded.

'That's awful. What happened to him?'

'The rope, as the law demanded.'

'And his wife?'

Titus looked grim. 'She escaped before I could arrest her and, mad for revenge, paid a nefarious old witch from Essex to lay a curse on Mary and strike her blind.'

Poor Mary, Hazel thought.

'I tracked them both down and dealt with them myself,' Titus said.

Hazel waited for him to continue, but he said nothing else. Eventually he refocused his eyes and fixed them on her.

'All of which,' he said, 'brings us back to you.'

Here it comes. Judgement, she thought. *Whatever happens, I'm not going to let him kill me without a fight.*

'No need to worry,' Titus said. 'I know a liar when I see one, and I'm satisfied you're no witch.'

Surprised but still suspicious, Hazel sat back. *Now I just need to find Bramley. Where is he?*

'Now we've cleared that up, we'll continue with the job you paid us for,' Titus said. 'We'll go and find your mother.' David snorted in disgust and went back to refilling musket cartridges. 'Now think hard – what did Murrell say to you back there in the forest? Did he give you any clue as to where she could be?'

'I have more than a clue,' Hazel said. 'I know exactly where they are.'

'You do?' Titus said. 'Where?'

'Rivenpike.'

Titus and David exchanged glances. 'Rivenpike,' Titus said. 'That forsaken place? I should have guessed.'

'People say it's cursed. No one goes there any more,' David murmured.

'Why not?' Hazel asked.

'The King made his last stand against Cromwell at

Rivenpike,' Titus said. 'When the siege was over, Cromwell sacked the place, and threw the surviving defenders off the cliff. It's been a ghost town ever since.' He glanced at David. 'Get me a drink, would you, boy?'

'We've a little coffee left. I'll boil some more water.'

'A proper drink,' Titus growled.

'We don't have anything left. You've quaffed it all.'

'All right, put the damn kettle on.' Titus turned to Hazel. 'To Rivenpike we go.'

Hazel swung her legs out of bed and looked around for her boots, impatient to get started.

'Mary had a familiar when I met her,' Titus said. 'A beautiful greylag goose. All Wielders have familiars, as I'm sure you know. Geese are common, as are cats, toads, dogs.'

Hazel straightened up, boots in hand, and fear starting its now customary crawl in her stomach.

Titus bent down and picked up a glass-sided box from under the table. 'Dormice too.'

Hazel stopped breathing. Trapped in the box with a face stricken with terror was Bramley.

24

THE SYPHON

*'For his services to the advancement of science and
invention I present Witch Finder Captain Titus White
with this master-crafted wrist-mounted pistol.'*
Simon Winters, Grand Master of the College of Witch Finders

'So you knew I was a witch all along?' Hazel fumed as David tied her to a chair.

Titus towered over her. 'Of course. Why else would a man like Murrell be interested in you? And despite my apprentice's various faults, I trust his word. I'm surprised you thought you could convince me otherwise.' He appraised her like a man deciding if a horse was worth his hard-earned money. 'Perhaps you're not as bright as I thought.'

Bright? I'm the stupidest girl who ever lived. Why did I ever think I could fool him?

David gave his knots an experimental yank.

'Ow!' she yelped, kicking out at him.

'Better tie her ankles too,' Titus said.

'Why bother? Why not just kill me now? That's your job, isn't it, Witch Finder?' she said as David lashed her feet to the chair legs.

'Don't presume you know me, girl,' Titus said. 'I'm letting you live. Although if you test my patience much further I might change my mind.'

'What do you want from me?'

'For now, I want you to be quiet and let me and the boy get on with our job.'

'To hunt my ma? Well, I won't let you. I'll—'

'Quiet,' Titus snapped. 'It's not her I want.' He sat down at the table, fists clenched. 'It's Murrell I'm after. David, bring me the map of Wychwood. We need to work out a route to Rivenpike.'

'Look,' Hazel said, 'if it's Murrell you want, let me help you.'

'We don't need help,' Titus said. He weighed down the map with books and then conferred quietly with David. Bramley stared helplessly at Hazel from his glass-fronted cage.

She craned her neck and noticed that a direct path to Rivenpike through the forest was shorter than the route the wagon would have to take by road. *If I can escape I can get to Rivenpike and find Ma first*, she thought. *But only if I can escape . . .*

Titus straightened up. 'Is that clear, boy?'

David nodded eagerly. 'We track this Murrell to Rivenpike and see what he's up to. And if we can, arrest him.'

'And what about my mother?' Hazel said.

David cast Hazel a poisonous look. 'She'll have to take her chances.'

Hazel embraced her anger like a long lost friend, feeling

hot magic flowing back into her veins.

'She's getting ready to cast,' Titus said, jumping to his feet. 'Get the Syphon, boy, quickly.'

David rummaged through the wooden trunk labelled 'Misc'.

Hazel recoiled as Titus grasped her chin in strong fingers. 'Anger's the trigger, isn't it?'

'Gerroff me,' Hazel spluttered. She tried to gather her magic but it felt slippery, impossible to grab.

'Where does it spring from?' He narrowed his eyes, as if trying to stare into her soul. 'Ah yes, your heart. It brims, doesn't it?'

'I can't find it, Boss,' David said, an edge of panic in his voice.

'It's there, under the telescope stand. Hurry up – she'll incinerate us both if you dither much longer.'

'Got it!' David hauled a glass tube banded with copper out of the trunk. At first Hazel thought it was some sort of telescope – until she saw the plunger at one end and a wicked looking needle sticking out of the other. It looked grotesquely surgical.

'. . . What's that?' she said.

Titus let go of her chin. 'I call it the Syphon,' he said, taking it from David. 'We can't have you using your magic on us.'

Hazel shrank back into her chair. 'You cowards – I don't even know how to use my magic.'

'We both know that's not true.' Titus pushed the plunger

156

down the tube with a sibilant hiss. 'And remember – I know what an accomplished liar you are.'

Before Hazel could reply, Titus pressed the blunt tip of the needle against her heart and heaved back on the plunger. Tongues of fire, red as blood, licked up the needle and filled the syringe. Hazel tried to scream as her magic leaked away, leaving her numb and shivering.

Titus handed the Syphon to David. It was full of bubbling orange liquid. She stared dazedly at it. *So that's what my magic looks like.* Her heart fluttered like a wounded bird.

As David locked it away in a trunk, Titus pressed a cup to Hazel's mouth. 'Drink,' he said.

You'll pay for this, she thought, glaring at him as she slurped the water.

The old Witch Finder turned to David. 'Get us moving. We've got a long journey ahead. Wake me at sunset and I'll take over the driving.'

David climbed through the hatch, closing it behind him as Titus collapsed on to his bunk. Soon his snores were mingling with the creak of the wagon.

It's now or never, Hazel thought. After a few deep breaths, she bunched her fists and strained against the ropes. The chair creaked and the rope's rough fibres bit her skin, but it was no use – she simply didn't have the strength. She slumped forward and closed her eyes.

Orange light filtered through her eyelids and warmth bathed her face, as if someone had opened a stove door. Bramley was standing with his front paws pressed against his cage door. Flames poured from his fur, licking against the glass.

That's it, my clever little mouse!

Clear rivulets of molten glass ran on to the table, blackening the wood, until Bramley had melted a hole big enough to wiggle through.

Hazel glanced at Titus. *Thank the sky he's such a deep sleeper.*

With startling agility, Bramley leaped across the table and landed on her lap. He mouthed, 'Hello,' and began to chew through the rope binding her left wrist. Hazel counted the seconds, forcing herself to sit motionless until the rope slithered to the floor.

She grinned with delight as Bramley scrambled up her arm and pressed himself against her neck.

'Took your time, didn't you?' she whispered.

He nipped her ear. 'Stop dithering and get the rest of those ropes undone.'

Eyes fixed on Titus, Hazel flexed some movement back into her fingers and set to work.

Slowly, agonizingly, she teased loose the knot around her other wrist. The second rope hit the floor. The chair creaked as she leaned down to untie her ankles. A lump of panic grew in her chest as the rope refused to loosen. *Come on, damn you!*

Bramley nudged her cheek. 'Slowly,' he murmured. 'Just take it slowly.'

Hazel closed her eyes, took a deep breath and went back

to working on the knots. Samson gave a whine and stood up.

'Hush, boy,' Hazel whispered, glancing nervously at Titus. 'Everything's all right.'

The coarse rope rubbed her fingers raw, but she didn't stop until they were all undone. She gripped the chair arms and stood up . . .

Cramp locked around her legs like a vice. She toppled forward, just managing to grab the table to keep herself from falling. It juddered across the floor, stopping an inch from Titus's outstretched leg. The tobacco jar teetered on the edge; Hazel was too slow to catch it. It crashed to the floor and rumbled into a corner. Titus stirred and rolled over.

Still propped up by the table, Hazel bit back a scream as fresh spasms seized her muscles, turning them into rockhard lumps of agony. Seconds scraped past. She risked putting her full weight on to her left leg, then her right. The cramp released its grip, leaving behind a dull throb. Keeping half an eye on Titus, Hazel picked up the map and tucked it under her arm.

The Grinder and a pair of Entropy Goggles glinted on the workbench. *They might come in useful*, she thought to herself. She unhooked her bag from the door and placed everything inside.

'Get that apple over there,' Bramley whispered. 'I'm starving.'

Hazel did as he asked, then opened the door and peered

outside. The air felt wonderfully cool. Late afternoon sunlight filtered through the branches, dappling the forest track with patches of gold. Freedom beckoned.

'Samson, be a good boy and stay,' she said.

The huge dog gave a whine but sat down obediently. Sighing with relief, Hazel leaped to the ground and scuttled into the trees. Crouching behind a holly bush, she watched the wagon disappear round a bend.

How long would it take for Titus and David to discover she had escaped? Would they turn back and try to capture her?

No point hanging around to find out, she thought. *Best get out of sight.*

25

THE RIVER WINDING

Experiments have shown that a Wielder spawns
magic from her corrupted bodily organs.
The English Witch Plague by Jacob Sprenger

'Well,' Bramley said from behind her ear, '*that* was close. I assume you've got fresh ideas on how to get us into yet more trouble?'

Hazel pushed through some trailing creepers. 'I'm working on a few.' She glanced over her shoulder to check that the road was out of sight.

Faded ribbons of sunlight trailed through the green canopy of branches. The air was warm, but Hazel hardly felt it due to the aching, magic-less void in her heart. She pulled her cloak tighter around her shoulders, cursing Titus and his Syphon.

'Do you think my magic will come back?' she said. 'I feel so cold without it. Sort of empty.'

'I don't know for sure, but I think it will over time. You'll just have to be patient.'

Hazel slid down a ditch, stepped over the sluggish brook at the bottom and climbed laboriously up the other side, noticing how much heavier her bag was now.

'So,' she said, 'tell me what happened back there in Mary's cabin.'

'Er . . . well, Titus came back after you'd foolishly fallen asleep. Then he put me in that confounded cage – after quite a struggle, I can tell you – and carried you out to the wagon,' Bramley said.

'Why didn't you try to warn me?'

'I . . . er—'

'You were asleep as well, weren't you?'

'I may have dropped off for a moment,' Bramley blustered.

'It's all right, Bram,' Hazel said, running her finger down his back. 'I'm only teasing.'

He burrowed deeper into her hair. 'I was so worried that they'd hurt you . . .'

'I know,' Hazel said. 'Let's not talk about it.'

Satisfied that they were far enough into the forest to be safe from pursuit, Hazel sat on a tree stump in a small clearing and spilt her bag on to the grass: tinderbox; bread (now rather hard); cheese (now rather mouldy); map; apple; Entropy Goggles and the Grinder.

Bramley hopped on to the ground and stood next to the apple.

'Hungry?' Hazel asked.

'A bit peckish. Although I don't think my teeth will ever be the same after cutting through all that rope.'

Hazel cut off a slice of apple. 'There – chew on that.'

Nibbling on some rock-solid bread, she laid the map on the ground. The title was printed in ornate gothic script across the top: *Wychwood and the Surrounds, in the Kingdom of England.*

The ink-washed forest spread across the parchment like a patch of green mould. As well as the villages, towns, lakes and hills, the mapmaker had added delicately rendered pictures of wolves, bears and deer. On the eastern edge was a walled city with a white tower and seven gates. It was labelled 'City of London'.

Hazel traced her finger over the network of roads and rivers, trying to work out where she was. 'This is Wormwood Lane, and there's Watley. So, I think we're here, by this river.'

Having polished off his apple slice, Bramley trotted over the map and sat on Plymouth. 'And where are we going?'

'Here.' Hazel pointed to a picture of a black tower. 'Rivenpike.'

'Where we'll find Murrell?'

'Yes.'

'And maybe Hecate?'

'I hope so.'

'But more likely our near-certain doom?' Bramley added, scratching at his tail with a paw.

'Quite possibly,' Hazel said with a grim smile.

Bramley snorted. 'How do we get there?'

'We find the river that leads to it,' Hazel replied.

'And how——?'

'By walking.' She scooped up Bramley and repacked her bag. 'And listening.'

When they found it, the river turned out to be narrow, weed-choked, and following a seemingly aimless course through the trees.

Night rose like black vapour, creeping up the trees and swallowing the sky. Hazel's breath misted and it wasn't long before her damp clothes were sticking to her like a second skin. Her legs ached; her back ached; everything ached. But worst of all, her heart still beat cold and empty.

'It's dirty back here,' Bramley said, breaking the silence. 'You need a wash.'

'Wash?' Hazel spluttered, tugging him out from behind her ear and dangling him by his tail. 'When am I supposed to find time to wash? I'm too busy getting us out of trouble.'

'*Into* trouble, more like,' Bramley said. 'Put me down this *instant*!'

'As you wish.' Hazel said, dropping him into the top of her bag and leaving him to sulk in silence.

She was beginning to wonder if she was following the right course when the river broke free from the confines of the forest and widened, tumbled and foamed towards a precipice. Hazel followed it out, picking her way between gorse patches and twisted saplings until the sky opened up overhead. Taking the last few steps carefully to avoid slipping on wet stones, she peered out over the precipice.

Below was a gorge, wide and deep, with sheer walls of jagged rock. Moonlight glinted on a river far below and the rush of water echoed between the cliffs. With an eerie hoot, a snowy owl swooped out of a nearby tree and glided down into the depths, outstretched wings shining like ivory as they cut through the air.

Bramley crept out from the bag and perched on her shoulder, their argument forgotten.

'Look,' he said. 'Over there.'

On the other side of the gorge, behind a screen of pine trees, rose the forbidding stone walls of a fortified town.

'Rivenpike,' Hazel breathed.

26
RIVENPIKE

After a month-long siege, Rivenpike has fallen. The Witch
War is over. England is free from the tyrannical King.
The *Daily Thunderer*, July 1644

Hazel stood at the end of a neglected bridge spanning the gorge to Rivenpike. On the other side was a half-ruined gatehouse with two towers studded with gun loops. The river churned far below.

Rivenpike's vast defensive wall was carved from solid rock, sweeping round the natural curve of the gorge. Narrow windows squinted between towers and flying buttresses, and from behind the topmost turrets peeked steep, grey-tiled roofs, gleaming like tarnished mirrors.

'No smoke from the chimneys and no lights in the windows. Looks abandoned, just like Titus said.' Hazel stepped tentatively on to the bridge. It groaned, as if deciding whether or not to bear her weight. Trying to ignore the dizzying drop, she risked the other foot.

'Rumour has it that some witches can fly,' Bramley said.

'Well, this one can't.' She grabbed the handrail, holding her breath as the bridge leaned with her. Inch by inch, she shuffled towards the middle of the span, feeling the structure shift and wobble under her.

There was a flash of white below. It was the snowy owl, drifting up the gorge with something dangling from its beak. *Death never sleeps*, Hazel thought, freezing as the wood under her feet cracked. *It just waits.*

'Why have you stopped?' Bramley squeaked.

'Bram?'

'What is it?'

'I want to apologize.'

'*What?*'

'I've taken you from your home and thrown you into terrible danger,' she said. 'And I've not thanked you once.'

'Do you really think this is the time?' Bramley's squeak was so high it was barely audible.

'Yes, because I might not get another chance,' Hazel said. 'Bram, you may be grumpy, and annoying, and rude, but thank you for sticking with me through all this danger.'

'I don't want your thanks, I just want you not to get me killed. Now, *hurry up.*'

Feeling a little lighter, Hazel edged her way to the other side of the bridge and paused under the gatehouse arch.

'We made it,' she said. 'Before we go on . . . is there anything you'd like to say to me?'

'No,' Bramley sniffed.

Hazel narrowed her eyes. 'Don't you want to apologize for the nasty things you said to me earlier?'

'My imperfect little witch,' Bramley said, pressing his warm body against her neck. 'There are two things you need to learn about dormice: we are always right, and we *never* apologize.'

Hazel shook her head in disgust. 'I give up.'

She crept out of the gatehouse on to a cobbled street. Terraces of grey stone buildings brooded on both sides, their windows dark and empty. A sign fixed to a shuttered tavern read 'Tower Road'. The road sloped up, winding its way towards a forbidding castle keep in the centre of the town.

'Look,' Bramley whispered. 'Mary was right. *Someone's* home.' Light glowed through the windows in the keep's topmost floors.

Hazel wondered with an aching sense of hope if her mother was in there. 'Let's take a closer look,' she said.

Silence pressed down on her as she crept up the street. Nothing moved except the silver-gilt clouds scudding across the sky. The shops and houses were as empty as nests in winter.

'You do take me to the nicest places,' Bramley said.

'I do my best.'

A sign reading 'Rumpole's Butcher – Cuts, Chops and Hocks' creaked in the breeze. Hazel peered through a smashed window at a counter and rows of bare shelves. A rat crouched on a marble chopping block, licking at a smear of dried blood.

'What happened here?' she wondered. 'Not even a ghost would want to stay in this awful town.'

She reached the top of the Tower Road, which opened

out on to a paved square of houses and shops. A dried-up fountain marked the centre.

Ahead loomed the castle keep, a blank witness to the life and death of the town it had been built to protect. The water in the surrounding moat looked as black as tar.

'It's huge,' Hazel said. 'It'll take forever to search it.'

'I don't know how we're even going to get inside,' Bramley said. 'The drawbridge is up.'

'We'll have to wait until someone lowers it and then sneak in,' Hazel replied. 'They'll have to come out at some point.'

'Brilliant. I was hoping to get captured again.'

'Do you have a better suggestion?' Hazel snapped.

There was a silence. 'I don't, no.'

'Well then.'

A wave of exhaustion crashed over her and she slumped in a doorway. She was cold, hungry, and hated the idea of just waiting around. An idea flashed into her mind when she saw a black slug gliding up the wall, leaving a sticky trail in its wake.

'Wait a minute . . .' She opened her bag and pulled out the Entropy Goggles. 'I could try these. They might give us a trail to follow.'

'A trail to a demon, not to your mother.'

Ignoring him, Hazel looped the strap over her head and settled the goggles over her eyes. The world turned misty and indistinct.

'I demand that you take those things off this *instant*!'

Bramley squeaked, scaling up her hair and trying to dislodge them from her face. 'No good can come of this.'

'I'm just looking, Bram,' Hazel said, fiddling with the levers.

'But it never stays "just looking" for long, does it?' Bramley huffed. 'Soon we'll be "just running" and "just screaming".'

Hazel flicked a lever at random and gasped as a glowing trail of green footprints appeared. 'Got some,' she said. 'Footprints leading from the keep up to that alleyway over there.'

Bramley clambered to the top of Hazel's head and squinted at the alley. 'How big are they?'

'The footprints? Oh, tiny. Petite, actually.'

'I don't believe you,' he said. 'You're don't really want to follow them, do you?'

'It's better than sitting here doing nothing,' said Hazel, pushing the goggles up on to her head and forcing Bramley to scurry for the safety of her shoulder.

'No,' Bramley squeaked. 'It most definitely is not.'

27
A STICKY END

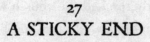

The alley wound between stone-and-timber tenement buildings. A single lantern hung from a wall, casting a feeble light that made the shadows deeper. *Another sign of life*, Hazel thought.

Ahead was a gateway with a wrought-iron sign arching over the top: 'Garden of the Dead – South Entrance'.

'Just when you think things can't get any gloomier,' Bramley said, 'we end up in a Garden of the Dead.' He paused. 'What exactly *is* a Garden of the Dead?'

'No idea.' Hazel stepped warily under the arch and out into a moonlit cemetery.

'Ah, I should have guessed.' Bramley sighed.

Using the goggles, Hazel followed the glowing green footprints up an avenue towards a large church with a clock tower. Rows of crypts, tombs and sarcophagi spread out in all directions, the pale stone bathing in moonlight and cut deep with shadows. A weeping stone angel gazed down with sorrowful eyes; Hazel sped past, half expecting it to move.

They had nearly reached the church when Hazel heard a swallowing sound followed by a loud belch. She ducked behind a tombstone and peeked out.

'What,' Bramley whispered, 'is *that*?'

Hazel raised the goggles. 'It's a demon. I recognize it from that book David showed me – a Shabriri, I think it was called. But what's it doing just sitting by the door?'

The demon bobbed up and down in a puddle of its own drool – at least Hazel assumed it was drool – licking its lips with a long black tongue. With its bulging eyes and green, warty skin, it resembled an overgrown toad.

'It looks like it's guarding the church.'

'Or guarding someone *inside* the church. It could be Ma.' Hazel's heart quickened.

'I suppose it's worth a look,' Bramley said. 'But how can we get past that Shabby-whatsit?'

Hazel grinned and pulled something out of her bag. 'Do you think I've just been lugging this around for fun?' she asked. Moonlight flashed on brass and silver.

Bramley squinted at it. 'The Grinder? Do you know how it works?'

Hazel turned it over in her hands. 'I *think* so . . .'

She poked her head around the edge of the tomb to study the Shabriri. An oily, fishy stink drifted in the air. *Does every demon have its own smell?* she wondered. *And are they always horrible?*

The Shabriri's bulbous eyes followed a moth as it blundered around the lantern hooked over the church door.

172

Faster than sight, the demon flicked out its tongue, caught the moth and pulled it into its mouth. Hazel grimaced as it crunched, swallowed and burped.

She put the Grinder on the ground. 'I need to enter the description. Shabriri is a *daemon-minimus*, so I press this lever. There ...' Mechanisms inside the Grinder clicked and whirred. 'Now, what are these levers? "Weight", "Height" and, er, "Disposition". What does "disposition" mean?'

'It means something's "propensity" or "constitution",' Bramley said smugly.

Hazel gave him a stern tap on the nose. 'I don't know what they mean either.'

'Ignoramus,' Bramley muttered. 'In words simple enough for *you*, "disposition" also means "temper", or "mood".'

'Thank you.' Hazel said. 'Well, it's just eaten, so I think the closest match is "Content".' She set the Grinder's levers using her best guesses, hoping that the demon's ears – *assuming it even has ears*, she thought – weren't sharp enough to hear. Then, as carefully as she could, she pushed it out into the avenue.

'Here we go ...' She pressed the 'Set Trap' lever then ducked back behind the gravestone. She stifled a yelp of surprise as five hinged brass levers tipped with blades rose out from the bowl-like centre of the Grinder and settled on the ground. With precise movements they scratched a five-pointed star filled with swirling patterns and writing into the stone.

'A magic circle,' Hazel whispered. 'How amazing!' She

couldn't imagine how a man like Titus could have made such a delicate contraption.

As the legs retracted back inside, the magic circle glowed and began to emit a thrumming that Hazel felt vibrating in her chest. *It must be letting off the aura that David told me about.* Unable to resist, she peeked out to see what the demon was doing.

'Careful,' Bramley said.

'Calm down, it can't see me.'

'Don't be foolish,' said Bramley. 'If *you* can see it, *it* can see you.'

Hazel pretended to ignore him but she did duck back a bit. With one eye, she watched the Shabriri stand up and sniff the air. The magic circle under the Grinder glowed even more brightly.

Come on, little fishy, Hazel thought. *Take the bait.*

The demon let out a thunderous burp and jumped high into the air with its powerful back legs. Hazel watched in fascinated horror as the Shabriri flew towards them and landed with a slap right next to the Grinder. She shrank back from its rotten-fish stench.

A green strand of drool leaked from its mouth and dangled like a pendulum as it leaned over to look inside. Hazel jumped as hinged blades sprang from the heart of the Grinder, plunging into the Shabriri and pulling it head first towards the rotating cogs at its centre. Within seconds the struggling demon was ground down to nothing more than a odorous pile of mashed flesh and bone.

'Well,' Bramley said, 'that was *disgusting*.'

'It worked though,' Hazel said, glowing with pride. 'I actually did it.' For the first time since leaving the Glade she felt as if she had really succeeded at something.

Hazel picked her way towards the Grinder and peered inside as the cogs slowed down and stopped. The blades were smeared with reeking oil, as was the ground around the device. Nothing remained of the demon; its earthly body had been destroyed and its soul flung back to the Underworld. 'Should we take the Grinder with us?' she wondered.

'Do you want to smell like a dead fish?'

Hazel nodded. 'Let's leave it.'

The key to the church was in the keyhole. Hazel lifted the lantern from its hook, unlocked the door and with a final backwards glance, slipped inside.

28
THE CHURCH AND THE BELFRY

Rebel demonologist Nicolas Murrell has escaped the Tower!
There is a bounty on the head of this enemy of the people.
The *Daily Thunderer*, August 1655

Hazel quietly closed the door and held up the lantern. The roof arched into a grey expanse of cold stone and chilly silence. Moonlight glinted through stained glass windows.

'It's empty.' Her whisper fluttered around the pillars and up into the roof beams.

Bramley crawled through Hazel's hair and perched on top of her head.

'Ouch! Careful – you're pulling my hair.'

'Stop fussing,' Bramley said. 'So, what is this place?'

'It's a church,' Hazel said, walking slowly down the aisle. 'Ma told me about them. Every town has one.'

'Oh. What are they for?'

'I'm not sure exactly. It's a sort of meeting place, I think. For singing and talking. And, er . . . worship. I think.' Hazel jumped as a pigeon burst out from under a pew and disappeared into the rafters.

'Who do they worship?' Bramley asked, crawling back

176

into her hair. 'It's a bit gloomy . . .'

'Enough questions, Bram. I'm trying to think.'

'No good asking you anyway, is it?' Bramley huffed. 'You don't know *anything*.'

Hazel sighed. He was right – there was so much about this land, and her mother's past, that she didn't know. That she might *never* know unless she could find her mother and escape. They stopped at the edge of a wide area of empty floor reaching towards the back of the church.

Hazel held up her hand. 'Hush! Can you hear that?'

'Hear what?'

'A sort of scratching sound.' The hairs on the back of her neck prickled. 'I think it's coming from . . . under the floor.'

'Don't be so sill—'

'Shh!' Hazel dropped to her knees and pressed her ear to the cool, gritty flagstones. There it was, scratching, barely an itch on the edge of her hearing, like claws against stone.

'There's something under there.' She stood up on wobbly legs. The scratching continued. 'Does this church have a cellar?'

'Look,' Bramley said. 'Everywhere is all dusty, but this bit of floor has been swept clean.'

'You're right – a spotless circle. And what's that?' She pointed to a white line running around the circumference. 'It looks like salt.'

'Something else to add to our tally of strange.'

Hazel wrapped her arms around herself as she crept

along the edge of the circle. 'It's getting colder, Bram. Can you feel it?'

'Of course I can,' Bramley squeaked. 'Let's go, can we, please?'

'One more minute. I want to make sure we haven't missed anything first.'

The pigeon took off and glided towards the back of the church, cooing softly as it landed on a pulpit. As Hazel followed its flight, a hatch in the wooden ceiling high above caught her eye. 'Perhaps I could get a better look from up there.'

Careful to stay outside the circle, Hazel sidled along the wall until she reached an arched doorway and a spiralling staircase leading into darkness. She paused for a moment, then started to climb.

'Sensible witches listen to their familiars,' Bramley grumbled.

'I do listen,' Hazel said, peering into the gloom. 'I just choose to ignore you.'

'Well, how about a bit of light so you don't fall and break your neck?'

Hazel stopped. 'You mean . . . use my magic? But what if it hasn't come back yet?'

'We just want a light to see by,' Bramley said. 'Not burn the place down. Just *try*.'

Hazel imagined a lantern glowing in the dark, and held the image in her mind's eye. Her cold heart throbbed painfully. 'I can't . . .'

'Listen to me,' Bramley said. 'You *can*. All you need is a spark. I know anger is where your magic came from – but other feelings can be powerful too. *Try again.*'

Hazel shut her eyes and thought of happy memories of her mother, the Glade and Mary. Her heart sent out a tiny pulse of warm magic, and her veins glowed like seams of gold.

One more little push . . .

She yelped with joy as flames burst from her fingers, lighting up the damp walls and, best of all, warming her up. With a mental push she made the flames flare up; and with a gentle pull they faded. Hazel did a delighted little jig.

'Not bad,' Bramley said. 'Not bad at all.'

Bursting with pride, Hazel held her hands in front of her. Shadows leaped on the walls, dancing to her whim. 'This feels amazing,' she breathed. 'I'm in control.'

'All right, bright eyes,' Bramley said, tugging her ear. 'We've got things to do, remember?'

Hazel grinned. 'Allow me to light the way.' She pulled back on her magic until only one hand was gloved in a flickering yellow glow. Keeping to the outside wall where the steps were widest, she continued to climb until she reached another low doorway. Floorboards creaked as she stepped into a wide, windowless room, seemingly without a ceiling.

'This must be the bell tower,' she said, flaring her magic and looking around.

Suspended on wooden mounts far above in the belfry

were the church bells. Ropes hung down, swaying in the restive air. A hatch lay open in the middle of the floor. Hazel drew in her magic as she approached, allowing the flames to shrink and disappear back under her skin. Slowly, carefully, she knelt down and peered over the edge.

29
THE MAGIC CIRCLE

A chill brushed Hazel's face, as if the hatch was exhaling a long, freezing breath.

'This cold isn't natural,' Bramley said, burrowing into the hair behind her ear. 'Where's it coming from?'

Hazel stared at the circular salt outline directly below. At first she couldn't focus; her gaze skittered over the floor as if her mind was unwilling to believe it was really there. Slowly, hard black edges appeared, strange patterns and jagged lines that hurt her eyes – and then, running around the circle's circumference, angular writing in a language she didn't recognize.

Hazel rolled on to her back and stared up into the belfry, feeling breathless and sick. 'It's a magic circle.'

'I don't like it,' Bramley said. 'We should leave. Whatever all this means, it's got nothing to do with us. Your mother's not here, so let's go before someone finds us.'

'You're right,' Hazel said, getting up and heading for the stairs. 'We've been here for too long. My curiosity will kill me one of these days. Oh, I could kick myself.'

'Kick yourself later. For now, just *hurry*.'

Hazel flew through the doorway and down the spiral staircase as fast as she could, using a little magic to light the way. Extinguishing the light, she scurried down the nave towards the front door.

'We should go back to the castle,' Bramley said.

'Good idea. We can—' Hazel froze with one hand on the door handle. 'Oh, hellfire! Someone's coming.'

'Didn't I tell you?' Bramley shrieked. 'You never listen!'

'Where shall I go?' Hazel whispered in a panic, running back the way she had come.

'Behind that stone table thing over there. *Quickly*.'

The voices were right outside the door. There was a click as the handle started to turn.

Hazel skirted around the circle – unable to bring herself to cross it despite her fear of capture – scampered up some steps and scrambled behind the altar just as the church door creaked open. Her heart hammered in her throat; she knew she was hidden from view, but she couldn't stop trembling.

Footsteps echoed – Hazel counted about ten or more sets. Were they all Murrell's followers? Lilith's silky voice rose over the noise, but Hazel couldn't make out what she was saying. Then it hit her: the tang of blood that she had grown to loathe.

Rawhead, she thought, burying her nose in the crook of her arm. *It's going to find me.*

'Hazel,' Bramley said. 'Stop whimpering. They'll hear you.'

'I can't help it.' Hazel curled her fingers into her hair and pulled until it hurt. 'I don't want to be eaten . . .'

'Calm down. I don't think they're here for you.'

'What about Rawhead? He can smell magic . . . and there's no way out.'

Bramley plopped on to her lap. 'That horrible circle thing is leaking magic like a rusty cauldron. That'll be more than enough to cloak your smell.'

Hazel picked him up and pressed his plump body against her cheek. 'Thanks, Bram.'

'Put me down,' he spluttered.

She put him back on her shoulder, took a steadying breath, then shuffled sideways towards the corner of the altar. 'Ready?'

'Ready for what?'

'I'm going to take a look.'

'Have you completely lost your senses? They might see you. It's this sort of reckless behaviour that got us into this mess in the first place.'

'I know,' Hazel said. 'But since we're already here . . . just a little peek?'

'I'll look first, and then tell you if it's safe to poke your fat, conspicuous head out. All right?'

Hazel resisted the urge to give him a kiss. 'Brave mouse,' she said, setting him on top of the altar.

She waited. Seconds ticked past, then, '*Psst!*' She looked

up and saw Bramley poking his head over the edge.

'It's safe to look,' he said, jumping down and burrowing into her hair. 'There are about ten witches gathering near the circle. Rawhead's prowling around, but there's no sign of Murrell.' He gave her a nip on the ear. 'I don't need to tell you to be careful, do I?'

'No, Bram, you don't.'

Hazel crouched on her haunches and cautiously peered out. She counted thirteen witches, ten women and three men, all clad in black floor-length robes. They stood around the circle, muttering to each other, their faces pinched with fear. Lilith stood a few paces apart, pale, beautiful, dressed in white. Rawhead prowled the circle, head down, sniffing at the salt.

Murrell's followers, Hazel thought. *I wonder why they're so nervous. And where are their familiars?*

Lilith raised her arms into the air and the other witches stopped whispering. 'Sisters and brothers,' she said, her voice cutting through the darkness. 'The moon is at its zenith. It is time for the summoning ceremony. To your places.'

'Oh dear,' Hazel muttered. 'I wonder what they're going to summon.'

'I don't know,' Bramley replied. 'But I don't think it's going to be friendly.'

30
THE SUMMONING

Demonology is the blackest of the magical arts,
practised only by the most dangerous witches.
The Infernal Magi *by Robert Boyle*

The witches spread out around the edge of the circle until they were an equal distance apart. No one spoke; tension filled the air until it seemed ready to burst. At a signal from Lilith each witch withdrew a fat tallow candle from their robes, placed it on the floor inside the salt boundary and then raised the hoods. Rawhead prowled in an endless circle, lips peeled back over curved teeth.

'Everything depends on us,' Lilith said. 'Whatever happens, do not stop the incantation. Recite the words exactly as we practised. A single mistake and all of our plans –' she blew across the palm of her hand – 'are dust in the wind.'

'What if it doesn't work?' a large witch with a bulbous nose asked. 'What if he's lost forever?'

'It *will* work, Tilda,' Lilith replied. 'Have faith. Now – begin.'

As one, the witches began to chant. It was an ugly noise, ebbing and flowing like a sluggish sea. Lilith threw back her head and cast a cold lament up to the rafters. All the candles burst into flame and mist seeped up through the floor, gathering inside the salt barrier like a pool of milk.

The air froze against Hazel's skin. Her breath fogged and she couldn't stop her teeth from chattering. She peered hard. What was that? The mist in the middle of the circle seemed to be bulging upward, as if something was growing underneath. The chant shrank to a whisper as the shape emerged. At first it was just an indistinct mass, but then details became clear: a fold of cloth, a battered boot, a twitching hand.

'It's a man,' Hazel said. 'But I can't see his face. The hood . . .'

The mist drained away, laying bare the circle with its pulsing magic sigils and the prone figure at its centre. Rawhead stood poised by the salt barrier, tongue flickering from between its teeth. A few witches lowered their hoods, exposing faces pinched with fatigue.

One of them stepped towards the circle. 'Quick, we must—'

'No,' Lilith cried. 'Stay outside. It's not safe yet.'

'But is it him?'

Lilith craned her head forward and smiled. 'It is.'

Bramley tugged on Hazel's ear. 'Who is it? I can't see.'

Hoping to get a better view, Hazel crawled to the other end of the altar. 'I'm not sure,' she said. 'But I can take a guess.'

'Murrell? But where's he just come from?'

186

Slowly, as if wary of hurting himself, the figure stood up.

'He looks different somehow,' Hazel said. When she had last seen him, Murrell had been middle-aged, tall and strong – but the man in the circle was bone-thin, stooped, and swayed on the spot as if the merest breath of wind would knock him over.

Lilith glided around the circle. 'Did you speak to our . . . patron?' she asked. 'Has he granted us what we desire?'

The figure drew back his sleeve. Scorched marks ran in lines all the way down his forearm. It looked like writing.

'Is that the spell?' Lilith asked, and when the figure nodded she held out her arms to him. 'Then your work is done. Come back to me, Nicolas. I will look after you now.'

31
DEMON BLIGHT

Speak not dark thoughts into the night,
For they lure dark beasts that scratch and bite.
The Sad Fate of the Pendle Witches by William Ward

'It can't be him,' Bramley squeaked. 'He looks completely different. He looks *old*.'

Lilith waited for Murrell to cross the salt before embracing him. The other witches approached cautiously, gathering around him in a loose circle; although stooped, Murrell still stood a head taller than most of them.

'My love,' Lilith said. 'Let me see your face.'

When Murrell spoke, his voice cracked like burning parchment. 'My friends, behold a man uniquely blessed –' and with shaking fingers he pushed back his hood to reveal his face.

Hazel knew with absolute certainty that she didn't want to look, but she couldn't help herself. Some of the witches gasped and stepped away. Lilith's hand fluttered to her mouth.

Murrell looked like death incarnate. Razor-thin lips. Sunken cheeks. Bald scalp. Skin laced blue with veins clung tight to his skull. He regarded his flock with maggot-hole eyes.

'It really *is* him,' Hazel whispered. 'Oh no . . .'

'What is it?' Bramley squeaked, cowering behind her ear.

'He's smiling.' Hazel closed her eyes but the image of Murrell's lips straining away from blackened teeth haunted her.

'It's as we feared – you've caught demon blight,' Lilith said, gently taking his arm. 'Let me take you to the healer.'

'The healer?' Hazel gasped.

'She must mean your mother,' Bramley said.

'My sweet consort, this affliction is a small price to pay for what I gained from our great patron,' Murrell said, stroking her cheek with long yellowed nails. 'I shall go to the healer . . . but there is something we must do first.'

Lilith lowered her head. 'As you wish, Nicolas.'

'Is there any sign of the girl?' Murrell asked. 'Or that Witch Finder she's taken up with?'

'No. Our familiars are out looking for them as we speak. Never fear, we'll find them.'

Hazel ducked back behind the altar, her heart pounding. 'We're too exposed here. We need to move.'

Bramley gnawed at his tail in frustration. 'But where can we go?'

Hazel pointed to the nearby pulpit – a raised platform enclosed with mahogany panels tall enough to hide behind. 'How about there?'

He frowned. 'I'll take a look first and make sure it's

suitable. Watch for my signal before you join me. Stay low, move quickly . . .'

'Thank you, Bram,' Hazel said, placing him on the ground.

The tiny mouse pressed himself to the floor and started a sort of sliding crawl towards the pulpit; he looked so ridiculous that if the situation hadn't been so dangerous, Hazel would have laughed.

Murrell continued his address. 'To seal the bargain, our patron, Baal the Destroyer, demands an immediate sacrifice,' he said. 'Did you find someone suitable while I was gone?'

Bramley reached the pulpit and hopped up the wooden steps. Hazel's heart missed a beat as he disappeared.

'We did, Nicolas,' one of the other witches replied. 'But perhaps if we brought the healer here . . . ?'

'No,' Murrell commanded. 'We must do as Baal wishes . . . *now*. Back to your places. The ritual must be completed.'

Baal must be a demon, Hazel thought as the Chosen scattered around the circle. *But what bargain has Murrell made with it?*

Bramley appeared on the rim of the pulpit, holding out his paw in her direction. Hazel identified a spot where the pulpit blocked the witches' line of sight. *I'll go there first*, she thought. *Then make a dash for it.*

'Bring the sacrifice to me,' Murrell commanded.

Bramley beckoned. Settling her bag more securely over her shoulder, Hazel dashed to the blind spot, keeping her head low and then skidding to a halt. She looked up, relieved to find that the pulpit did indeed hide her from the gathered witches.

Murrell's voice drifted through the church. 'Ah, there she is. Good, good.'

Hazel was about to creep the final yards to safety when all of Bramley's fur stood on end. He pointed towards the ceiling. Hazel followed his finger and her blood turned to ice water.

32

A POOR MAN'S LUCK

Lupus est homo homini *[Man is wolf to man]*
Anon.

Spindle slid as silently as a shadow between the roof beams, feeling its way on long, multi-jointed legs. The spider-demon stopped over the circle – its bulging eyes and fangs lit up by a shaft of moonlight.

Exposed in the middle of the chancel, Hazel felt like a fly trapped in a web. An image of David being smothered under the spider's bloated body paralysed her as effectively as any venom. Bramley beckoned to her with both paws, his eyes bright with fear.

Hazel willed her legs to work, and after a few shaky paces her courage ebbed back. She sped up, keeping her eyes on Bramley, expecting Spindle to drop to the ground and scuttle towards her at any moment. But luck was on her side, and before she knew it she was inside the pulpit, hunkered down in the cobwebby gloom.

Bramley plopped down on to the floor and Hazel gathered him up and held him to her chest.

'About time,' Bramley said. 'I thought you were going to sit there all day.'

Being careful not to make a sound, Hazel stood up and peered over the rim of the pulpit. She knew it was risky, but at least an angled bookrest built on to the front panel hid her from the spider-demon.

Murrell, Lilith and Rawhead stood on the other side of the circle. The rest of the witches were back in their places around the edge. They were all looking up at Spindle, and the thread-swaddled cocoon dangling from its spinnerets. Hazel's scalp crawled when she saw that it was about the size of a man, and it was wriggling.

Spindle's abdomen pulsed as it let out more thread to lower the cocoon into the middle of the circle.

'Is it safe to enter?' Lilith asked.

Murrell nodded, scratching absently at his scarred arm.

Lilith drew out a knife, crossed the salt and knelt by the captive. 'It would be to your advantage to stop moving,' she said, then set to work slicing through the layers of thread.

'Where did you find him?' Murrell asked.

'In a cabin near Watley,' one of the witches replied.

Murrell grunted. 'The Witch Hunters purged Watley not long ago.' He gazed down at the now-still captive. 'I wonder if he lost anyone?'

Lilith pocketed the knife and pushed her fingers through the layers of thread. There was a dry rip as she peeled the silk away, revealing a man's head. His face was without expression, but his eyes darted all around.

'Bram!' Hazel gave a gasp. 'I think it's the woodsman.'

'He must be the unluckiest man who ever lived.' Bramley fidgeted. 'We can't help him. I know it's a horrible thing to say, but we just can't. We have to pick our fights – pick the ones we *can* win. Us getting killed won't help your mother.'

'Lift him up,' Murrell said, a light burning somewhere in the depths of his eyes. 'He deserves to hear this standing on his feet.'

Lilith and one of the other witches hoisted the woodsman upright. He lolled between them, head drooping as if his muscles had been severed.

'I can see that you are a man of humble means,' Murrell said, circling the woodsman. 'Your life is of no consequence to anyone except you, and those close to you. But I am giving you a chance to make a difference to the *world*, a chance to do some good.' The woodsman swallowed and let out a strangled croak. Murrell stopped in front of him. 'Speak, if you can. I'm listening.'

'What are you going to do to me?' The woodsman's words were slow and slurred, as if too big for his mouth.

'I am going to let a demon consume your soul.'

The awful incomprehension in the woodsman's eyes was almost too much for Hazel to bear.

'But why . . . ?' he asked.

'I do it because I *must*.' Murrell gestured to the witches in the circle. 'Put him down and go back to your places.'

194

They left the woodsman lying helplessly on his back, too feeble even to turn over.

'Prepare to perform the containment spell, and *whatever happens*, don't stop,' Murrell commanded, raising his arms. 'Sisters and brothers – begin!'

33
WRAITHS

The King was kept in Carisbrooke Castle for some years
until his execution. Cromwell often visited him to gloat.
The Secret Diaries by Lady Catherine Coe

The words of the chant created a thick, impenetrable noise. The candles flared, deepening the shadows. Murrell swayed in time to the chant's heartbeat-pulse, his outline becoming blurry – as if he was standing behind a rain-streaked window. Colours of every shade slid up from the salt barrier, swirling like ink on water.

'They've sealed the circle with magic,' Bramley said. 'That poor man is trapped.'

The woodsman rolled on to his stomach and somehow found the strength to crawl towards the edge of the magic circle. Unable to help, Hazel bit her lip and forced herself to watch.

Murrell lifted up his sleeve and recited the words branded on his arm. It was not English; indeed, it didn't sound as if it could be *any* human language. Although their meanings were unknown to Hazel, she knew from the nausea roiling in her stomach that they spoke of pain and suffering.

In the roof far above, Spindle quivered. Rawhead paced in an endless circle.

The floor inside the salt barrier rippled like liquid. Hazel saw something glide underneath, then five sinuous tentacles broke through the surface, uncoiling, undulating, feeling the air with their delicate tips.

'What are they?' Bramley squeaked. 'Is that one creature or five?'

Hazel was too horrified to reply. The tentacles were already ten feet high, with thick, muscular roots. The woodsman glanced over his shoulder. His eyes widened. He gasped. Then he screamed.

The tentacles whipped round, and in the time it took for a heart to beat twice they were on him. Two around his ankles, two around his wrists, and with a yank he was on his feet. The fifth tentacle – thicker than the others – reared up like a cobra and swayed hypnotically from side to side. There was a wet tearing sound as its tip peeled open like a flower, revealing a round, toothless throat. The woodman went rigid as it descended towards his head.

Hazel's courage dissolved and she slid to the floor, pressing her hands over her ears in a vain attempt to block out the woodsman's muffled shrieks.

'See?' Murrell cried. 'See how his soul is being drawn out? Now watch, when Baal has feasted . . . Yes, he's *changing*. Demonic gifts are being bestowed. Keep chanting, my friends – our new brother may need taming before we set him free.'

Using every ounce of courage she possessed, Hazel peered back out from the pulpit.

The tentacles now stood straight up, swaying like reeds in a pond. They had turned from grey to washed-out pink – *Was that the colour of the woodsman's soul?* Hazel wondered – and as she watched, they gradually sank through the floor and disappeared.

The magic barrier made everything blurry but Hazel could see that the woodsman was still there. He stood with his back to her, head bowed and shoulders moving slowly in time with each deep breath. He looked broader, stronger, and Hazel sensed a menace in his stillness that frightened her.

The magic barrier crackled as Murrell pressed his hand against it. 'Can you speak?' he asked the silent woodsman. 'Do you remember your name? Do you remember anything at all?'

The woodsman said nothing.

'It seems not,' Murrell murmured. 'Baal has granted me power to command you.' He raised his arms. 'Cease the containment chant. Our new brother will not harm us.'

Lilith sidled up behind him. 'Are you sure, Nicolas? Can you really control it?'

'Do you doubt Baal's word? Do you doubt *me*?'

'No, it's just—'

'Then do as I say.' Murrell looked at Lilith through narrowed eyes. 'I find your lack of faith disturbing.'

Lilith slunk away and sat at the end of a pew.

198

'They don't seem to be getting on so well,' Bramley muttered.

The chant faded and the candlelight went from red to yellow. The barrier wavered and disappeared. Most of the witches backed away, watching the woodsman warily.

Hazel remembered the man she'd met on the fringes of the forest, the man with so much weariness and grief etched into his face. All that had gone and been replaced with a terrible dead-eyed stare.

'Hazel,' Bramley whispered. 'Whatever you do, don't sneeze.'

Hazel ducked down into the pulpit. 'What?'

'Don't sneeze. I don't want you to give us away. So don't sneeze.'

'Stop saying that – it makes me think I want to,' Hazel hissed, suddenly aware of all the dust. It was everywhere – carpeting the floor, floating in the air, covering her clothes . . . A tickle struck deep inside her nose. She closed her eyes, fighting the irresistible urge to let go and explode.

Bramley slid head first down her forehead, landed on her nose and clamped his paws against her nostrils. 'Don't you dare,' he hissed.

Hazel closed her eyes and let out a long, shaky breath. 'Better now,' she muttered, lifting Bramley back into her hair. With a final precautionary rub of her nose, she peeked back out.

'He feels no fear, no pain, and is not troubled by conscience,' Murrell said as he hobbled around the woodsman. 'He is a soldier under my command, a soldier who will fight to the death; and with an army of them I will bring Cromwell and all Witch Hunters to their knees. Do you trust me to lead you to freedom?'

'We do,' Lilith cried, and the others nodded enthusiastically.

'Thank you,' Murrell said. 'Because without you by my . . .' He put a hand to his forehead and swayed.

Lilith grabbed an arm to steady him. 'It's time to take you to Hecate. *No arguments.*'

Murrell smiled and allowed her to lead him down the aisle. The witches, the demons and the poor woodsman, now Murrell's newest servant, followed.

'They're leaving,' Hazel said. 'Come on. Let's go and find Ma.'

34
THE CASTLE

'Every Witch Finder must employ an apprentice.'
Charles Stuart, King of England, Scotland and Ireland, 1636

Hazel breathed in the crisp night air. After being trapped in the church for so long, it was good to be outside and on the move. *No more just watching and hiding,* she thought as she crept between the graves. *It's time to actually do something.* It felt like a lifetime had passed since she'd arrived in Rivenpike, but she supposed it had only been a couple of hours.

She peered down the alley. The witches were already out of sight, leaving only their shadows behind on the walls. Hazel followed, blood pumping, until she turned the final corner. Ahead, bathed in moonlight, lay the market square and the castle.

The witches gathered around Murrell by the lowered drawbridge leading into the keep. Hazel dashed over to a horse trough and ducked behind it.

'Careful,' Bramley snapped. 'You're too close.'

'They can't see through stone.' After a few frustrating moments Hazel snorted in disgust. 'It's no good, I can't

201

hear what they're saying.'

'Let me have a go,' Bramley said, hopping from her shoulder on to the edge of the trough. 'I've got better hearing than you.'

'Do you? You've never mentioned it.'

'There are a lot of things I'm better at than you,' Bramley said with a sniff. 'But I don't like to show off.'

'Hmmm. So, what are they saying?'

'Murrell's ordering them all to gather their familiars and go out and bring back more people for Baal. And they're to take the woodsman with them.'

'What else? Anything about Ma?'

'Oh dear,' Bramley squeaked.

'What?'

'Oh dear . . . *oh dear.*'

'What? *What?*'

'They're talking about us. Well, you, really. He's telling Rawhead to hunt you down. He suspects you might be nearby, trying to find Hecate.'

'We need to get into that castle,' Hazel said, watching the witches and the woodsman disappear down Tower Road; Murrell, Lilith and Spindle were already halfway across the drawbridge.

'So what's your plan?'

'We follow Murrell and Lilith and hope they don't see us.'

There was a clank as the drawbridge chains drew tight.

'Quick,' Bramley said. 'They're raising the bridge.'

Hazel launched herself across the courtyard, bag banging against her shoulder, arms pumping at her sides. Wood creaked as the drawbridge cleared the ground; the castle keep was closing its jaws. She forced her tired legs to go faster, knowing she only had seconds before it was out of reach.

'Go, go, go!' Bramley squeaked.

Her lungs pumped like bellows and it felt as if her feet hardly touched the ground. Twenty paces away, ten paces, five . . .

Fearing it was already too high, Hazel jumped. The air whooshed from her chest as she collided with the end of the bridge. Legs kicking and too panicked to feel any pain, she clawed at the wood, searching for something to grab hold of. Her fingers fumbled over a crack between the beams and, with a sideways swing, she managed to hook her leg over the end of the bridge and haul herself up. But she wasn't safe yet.

The bridge was nearly closed and in a few more seconds she'd be crushed between it and the stone tower. She looked down at the ever-steepening slope to the ground and, with only half a breath's hesitation, let herself roll. Everything spun, faster and faster, until she came to a bruised and gasping halt in a puddle of rainwater.

The drawbridge juddered shut with a clank of chains.

Hazel lay still, as water soaked into her clothes. Everything hurt: her ankle throbbed, her elbows were sore, and her head felt battered and woozy. But through it all she savoured the fierce joy of victory: she was another step closer to her mother.

'Bramley?' she croaked.

He stirred in her hair. 'I'm not speaking to you.'

'Fine,' Hazel said, crawling behind a pile of barrels. 'As long as you're all right.'

'I'm not all right. *That's* why I'm not speaking to you.'

'Don't be such a grump. We're still alive, aren't we?'

Rubbing her skinned elbows, Hazel waited for the aches and pains to subside and her brain to start working again. As her eyes adjusted she peered through a gap between the barrels and saw she was in a high-vaulted chamber with swords, spear tips and bits of armour lying in jumbled piles. A nearby door opened. Inside were iron cogs, pulleys and coils of chain.

The drawbridge mechanism, she thought.

Murrell and Lilith emerged holding flaming torches, followed by Spindle. They disappeared through a large door on the far side of the chamber. After giving them a head start, Hazel tucked her hair behind her ears, pulled up her hood, and followed them. After peering around the door frame to ensure they were nowhere in sight, she crept into a vaulted banqueting hall.

A long table lay upended in the middle of the floor. Plates, candelabras, discarded weapons and broken chairs lay strewn everywhere. Everything was covered in a thick layer of dust. A tapestry hung forlornly over a fireplace, the once striking scene of jousting knights now engulfed in mould.

'This must be where the final battle of the Witch War took place,' Hazel whispered.

Lilith's voice drifted from somewhere above. Floorboards creaked. Following the noise, Hazel headed for a sweeping staircase leading to a balcony overlooking the hall. Keeping her back to the wall, she edged up the steps until she reached the top. A faint light glowed from one of the many doorways, reflecting on stone steps spiralling up into darkness.

35

DON'T LOOK DOWN

'Magic and demons are closely connected;
thus, all witches are tainted with evil.'
Witch Hunter Captain Daniel Abnett

Through the door and up the stairs she went, quickly, quietly, not daring to use her magic for fear of giving herself away. Doorways gave out to deserted corridors, home now only to shadows and dust. Wind whistled through narrow windows as she followed the light ever upward, until she thought her legs would give way beneath her.

After one more twist of the staircase she found herself in a small square room with arrow slits in the walls. A doorway led outside.

'This must be where we saw the light shining from,' Hazel said, padding over to the door. Outside lay the castle's windswept battlements. Squat towers rose up from each corner. The door leading inside the opposite tower was closed – and there was a crack of light showing at the bottom.

There they are, Hazel thought.

Leaning into the buffeting wind, she skirted the edge of the roof until she reached the tower. Muffled voices came from inside.

'Quick, get out of sight,' Bramley squeaked from behind her ear. 'They could come out any minute.'

'Hush, mouse,' Hazel said, pressing her ear to the door. 'I'm trying to listen.' She closed her eyes and concentrated. 'It's Murrell's voice, but I can't hear what he's saying.' She leaned over the battlements. A little way away, light spilt from a window in the tower, and there was a narrow ledge against the outside wall running right underneath it.

Oh well, Hazel thought, hopping up on to the wall, sitting down and dangling her legs over the edge. *Here goes.*

'No, no, no!' Bramley squeaked in horror. 'Even you wouldn't be stupid enough . . .'

Hazel closed her eyes, slid off the wall and let herself drop.

A feeling of weightlessness, a second of panic, a sickening lurch in her stomach, and then her feet hit the ledge. She felt the solid stone under her feet and pressed her back against the wall as hard as she could. The wind tugged her cloak and whipped her hair. After a few seconds to gather her courage, she took a tentative sidestep towards the window.

Bramley was so agitated he'd tangled himself up in her hair. 'Oh, you stupid girl! Go back . . . No! Don't move. Don't look down . . . Oh, what have I done to deserve such intolerable treatment?'

Ignoring his frantic tugs and keeping her back flat to the wall, Hazel sidestepped with her left leg, and after testing the foothold slid her right leg along to meet it. The ledge was solid – but it was slippery too, and years of erosion had worn the edge to a slope.

Step after step and still the window didn't seem to get any closer. She risked a glance down at the drop. Dizziness swooped from her head to her stomach and for a heart-stopping moment she felt herself tipping into the void before her.

She fixed her eyes on the horizon and took a deep, steadying breath. The sky above the edge of the world was turning blue and chasing the scattered stars away. Dawn was about to break. When she thought that her sense of balance had returned, Hazel continued her laborious journey, never once thinking about turning back.

At last she reached the edge of the window. It was small, barred, and set in a deep, narrowing recess in the wall. As quietly as she could, Hazel dropped to all fours and crawled inside. Through the bars lay a candlelit room – probably once a guard's chamber – with a bed, a bench running along the wall, and a basin of water in the corner.

Hecate sat on the end of the bed, straight-backed with her red hair burnished in candlelight. She had one hand resting on a cage, and squeezed inside with his hackles poking through the bars was Ginger Tom. Hazel could barely stop herself from crying out with joy.

'So Rawhead did find him when he went back to the Glade,' Hazel whispered, glad that Hecate and her familiar were together.

'Much as I dislike that cat, I hope he gave that demon a scratch or two before he was caught,' Bramley said.

Hazel followed her mother's glare and saw Murrell leaning heavily against the door. He looked even worse than he had in the church – the journey up the tower had clearly taken its toll. Lilith was placing their torches in sconces on the wall.

Tom gave a furious hiss, his baleful eyes turned towards the ceiling. Hazel flinched when she saw Spindle, clinging upside-down in a corner and looking even more grotesquely enormous in the confines of the room. Its fangs mashed the air, shiny with venom.

'I need your help,' Murrell said, lowering his hood to reveal his ravaged face.

'Demon blight,' Hecate gasped. 'You're riddled with it. Is this why you went to so much trouble to find me? So I could cure you?'

'It was . . . one of the reasons, yes.'

Hecate shook her head. 'You were always reckless, Nicolas, but you were never a fool.'

Lilith took a step forward, her hair frosting with magic. Hecate didn't even flinch.

Murrell glanced at Lilith. 'Leave us. I wish to speak to the healer in peace.'

Lilith's face crumpled and her magic faded away. 'But—'

'Take Spindle and search Rivenpike – that Witch Finder may be sniffing around.' He cast a wry glance at Hecate. 'And as for the girl, if she's as persistent as her mother – fear of death won't stop her from coming here. If she's hereabouts, I want her captured.'

Lilith cast Hecate a venomous glare and stormed out. With a hiss, Spindle squeezed its swollen body through the door and followed its mistress. Murrell smiled ruefully as he closed the door and slumped on to the bench, clasping his cane in gnarled fingers.

'You've seen Hazel?' Hecate said quietly.

'I have.'

'Where was she?'

'Somewhere in Wychwood. She's looking for you.' Murrell smiled. 'You don't know whether to be proud, angry or frightened for her, do you?'

'I'm her mother. I'm all of those things.'

'She won't give up until she finds you. Despite Rawhead, despite Spindle . . . despite even me.'

'If you hurt her—'

Murrell held up a hand. 'I have no wish to harm your child, Hecate, but she is a powerful Wielder, and stubborn. If she tries to rescue you, or puts any of my followers in danger, I will do what I have to.'

'She's just a little girl!'

Not any more, Hazel thought. *I'm a Fire Witch. I've become what you feared I would, Ma.*

'You underestimate her,' Murrell said with a tremble in his voice. 'She's loyal. More loyal than you ever were.'

'The war was lost, Nicolas. You just wouldn't admit it.'

'You abandoned us!'

Hecate pressed her hands against her stomach. 'I was expecting a child. I had to think of her before anything else. Surely you can understand that?'

Murrell's anger faded, as if he didn't have the strength to sustain it.

'You should have told me about her,' he said. 'Everyone loved you, Hecate, and if we'd known you were with child we'd have fought all the harder to protect you both. Perhaps hard enough to win.'

'You deceive yourself. I am sorry for it, but I know I made the right choice.'

Murrell gazed into the fire. 'We lost all hope when we realized that you had gone. That was the day we lost the Witch War.'

Hecate leaned forward and took his fragile hands in hers. 'Let me go. Let me find my daughter and go home. We've no part to play in your plans—'

'Yes, you do. *Both* of you,' Murrell snapped, pulling away. 'Hazel's fire-magic is a powerful weapon that I can use in the coming war, and I *am* going to find her. In the meantime, I'm offering you a chance to atone.'

'What does "atone" mean?' Hazel whispered.

'It means "to make amends",' Bramley replied.

'You want me to cure you?' Hecate asked.

Torchlight fell on Murrell's face as he leaned back against the wall. His skin looked transparent in the torchlight. 'That is why I went to so much trouble to find you.'

'The plan you've hatched with that demon is evil.'

'It's our only hope of survival. When I told you about it, I'd hoped you would understand—'

'If I help you, how many innocent people will you sacrifice in that dreadful ritual?'

'Enough to build an army strong enough to defeat Cromwell and all his Witch Hunters. Then we can undo all the lies told about our people and make England a place where magic and non-magic folk can live in peace.' Murrell ran a shaking hand over his face. 'But first, sacrifices must be made.'

Hecate bit her lip. 'You're walking in the dark now, Nicolas, and I don't think you'll ever find your way out.'

Murrell's voice cracked like glass. 'If you don't help me, you condemn me.'

'You condemned yourself to this disease when you consorted with a demon. You knew the risks.' She shook her head. 'No, I won't cure you, and I won't help you carry out your plan.'

Murrell watched Hecate closely for a moment before painfully hauling himself to his feet. 'I *will* find your daughter – have no doubt about that. And when I have her, you *will* do what I say.'

The door closed. There was the click of a key turning in the lock and then the *tap tap tap* of Murrell's cane fading across the rooftop. Hecate sat on the bed, head bowed, worrying the hem of her dress between her fingers.

'Well?' Bramley whispered, tugging gently on Hazel's ear. 'What are you waiting for?'

Hazel reached through the bars. 'Hello, Ma,' she said.

36

DARK DESCENT

'In return for Royal Patronage, all witches do make this solemn
oath: To help the people; to protect the land; to do no harm.'
Oath given by Sarah Lilly, First Witch of the Coven,
to Queen Elizabeth Tudor, 1570

Hecate looked up and gasped. 'Hazel? No ... no ... *no!'*
She scrambled backwards across the bed and
tumbled over the other side, dragging the blankets with her.
'What are you?' she cried. 'Some demon in false form, sent
to torment me?'

'Don't shout,' Hazel pleaded. 'It really is me. Look at
Tom – *he* knows who I am.' Ginger Tom was watching
Hazel from his cage, rubbing his flanks against the bars and
purring loudly.

Hecate untangled herself from the blankets. 'Tom, is
that really ... my daughter?'

The cat gave a series of miaows and chirrups. Hecate
listened, her wide eyes never leaving Hazel.

Something burst inside Hazel. Her face scrunched up
and, without warning, tears began to flow down her cheeks.
'Ma, it's me, so please just give me a hug.'

Hecate bounced across the bed, nearly knocking Tom's
cage to the floor. 'My dear, sweet daughter ... I'm so sorry.'

Hazel glowed as her mother drew her tight to her chest – it felt as if the bars between them had melted away.

'It's really you. Nicolas said you were on my trail. He's out trying to find you . . . and you were here the whole time?'

Hazel nodded, smiling and laughing and wiping away her tears. 'I heard everything . . .'

Hecate's eyes strayed to the edge of the windowsill, just inches behind Hazel. Her face slackened with horror. 'You've been crawling around out there on the *ledge*? Don't you realize how high we are? You could have fallen. You could have been *killed*.'

Bramley tugged at Hazel's ear. 'That's what *I* said.'

'I have excellent balance,' Hazel said. 'Besides, I just *had* to know if it was really you in here.'

'Come in here at once, Hazel Hooper, so I can scold you properly.'

Hazel examined the bars across the windows. 'I might not be able to get through these, but I can probably deal with the door. And before you say it, yes, I'll be careful.'

Hecate gave Hazel a squeeze. '*Be careful*,' she whispered, and then reluctantly let her go.

Hazel rolled her eyes and crawled on to the ledge. 'Ma worries too much,' she said, inching her way back to the rooftop.

'Don't be churlish,' Bramley said. 'Would you rather she didn't worry about you at all?'

Hazel mumbled something indistinct.

'Pardon?' Bramley said. 'I couldn't hear you.'

'I said, I suppose not.'

Hazel carefully edged her way back along the ledge to the rooftop. After checking the coast was clear, she scurried across the flagstone roof and knocked on the stout wooden door. 'Ma, stand away.'

She pressed her palms against the door and soon the wood was smouldering and turning black. Smoke and flakes of ash curled away on the breeze. This time she barely had to concentrate to control her magic. It was a bit like moving her limbs – she wanted it to happen, and it just . . . did.

Wielding isn't as painful as it was, she thought. *It's starting to feel easier.*

Flames crackled as her hands pushed right through the planks, and then the handle and lock mechanism fell to the floor with a clank. The door flew open and Hazel tumbled into her mother's waiting arms.

'So, you really are a Fire Witch,' Hecate whispered, holding Hazel so tightly that she could barely breathe. There was a catch in her voice – half proud, half sad.

Hazel nodded. 'I always knew I was just like you. Magic was in me all along, but it took that demon hurting you to spark it in me.'

'Magic and emotions are connected,' Hecate said, drawing back to look her daughter in the eye. 'But listen to me. Being a Wielder is dangerous. People will either want to use you . . . or kill you.'

'I know, Ma,' Hazel said. 'I've seen enough of England to

215

know the truth now. But we won't let them hurt us, will we?'

Hecate kissed the top of her head. 'No, we won't.'

'First we need to get out of this castle,' Hazel said, crossing the room to peer out of the window. 'But the drawbridge is closed and Murrell, and Lilith and that horrible demon of hers are still in the castle somewhere.'

'I know a secret way out,' Hecate said. 'It was built during the war, and was known only to the Queen and her closest confidants.'

'So how do you know about it?'

Hecate gave a secretive smile.

'You knew the Queen?' Hazel asked in disbelief.

'Indeed I did. But listen, I'll tell you all about it when we're safe,' Hecate said. 'For now, can you get Tom out of his cage?'

'No! Leave him in there,' Bramley squeaked.

'I think so,' Hazel said, kneeling by the bed and pressing her finger and thumb around the lock. Tom backed away, hissing as it glowed red under her touch.

'Careful, don't burn yourself,' she said to the cat as the lock melted into a puddle of liquid metal.

The door swung open and Tom leaped out, rubbed himself against Hazel, and then jumped into Hecate's arms, purring contentedly.

'Good boy, Tom, good boy,' Hecate murmured.

A wave of dizziness overcame Hazel as she stood up and she grabbed the bedspread to steady herself.

'You've overdone it,' Hecate said, helping her towards the door. 'You need to be careful not to use your magic up all at once.'

'But it *will* come back?'

'Yes. And it will come back stronger. Your ability to cast magic is like a muscle – as you exercise it, it will get stronger. You're going to be a very powerful Wielder, my girl.'

'You sound sad.'

'I am. You'll always be in danger now.'

'Great,' Bramley muttered dolefully from behind Hazel's ear.

'Are you ready to show me your way out?' Hazel asked.

Hecate put Tom down and pulled on a hooded cloak. 'Yes, it's this way.' She took Hazel's hand and led her across the rooftop and into one of the other towers. Tom bounded ahead, his magnificent orange tail standing straight up in the air.

'I can't believe you followed me here,' Hecate said. 'And on your own, too.'

'I wasn't alone,' Hazel said. 'I'm here with Bramley.'

Hecate paused at the top of the stairs. 'Hazel,' she beamed. 'Are you trying to tell me that you have your own familiar? That's wonderful! Can I meet him?'

'He's a bit shy . . .' said Hazel, as Bramley scrabbled forward and peered out of her mass of red curls. 'Ma, this is Bramley.'

Bramley squeaked and gave a little bow.

Hecate bent down to look at him. 'Why, we've met

before. Hello again, Master Mouse. How's the paw?'

Bramley held it up and waved.

'Good, good,' Hecate said. 'So, you've been looking after my Hazel, have you?'

He gave a shy nod.

'I think you'll find I've been looking after *him*,' Hazel said.

Bramley cast Hazel an indignant glare, before darting back into her hair as Tom miaowed hungrily.

'No, you may not eat this mouse,' Hecate snapped at him. 'I don't care,' she carried on over a chorus of increasingly disgruntled miaows. 'He's Hazel's familiar. Yes, you will do as I say!'

'That horrible cat,' Bramley quivered. 'I'll take Rawhead any day.'

They descended the stairs, deeper into the dark, until they reached the ground floor and an arched stone corridor dripping with moisture.

'Nearly there,' Hecate said, lifting up her cloak and hopping daintily over the puddles.

'Is there another drawbridge then?' Hazel asked, splashing after her.

'No.'

'Then how are we going to cross the moat?' Hazel asked.

'We're going to swim.'

'Ah, now I know where you get your sense of humour from, Hazel,' Bramley said.

Hecate sighed. 'I remember this place when it was the

King's stronghold, full of courtiers, soldiers, and witches with their familiars.'

Hazel stopped mid-puddle, knowing this was not the time for awkward questions, but unable to stop herself. 'Why didn't you tell me about all this? About Murrell, and you fighting in the Witch War, and running away with me?'

Hecate glanced at her, her face unreadable in the gloom. 'I wanted to protect you. I'm your mother – that's my job.'

'You should have told me the truth about your past.'

Hecate folded her arms. 'The past doesn't concern you. What happened in that dreadful time is between me and . . .'

' . . . Murrell,' Hazel finished. A question that had previously never occurred to her rose to the surface of her mind, making her cold and sick to her stomach. She looked at her mother's dark outline and asked, 'Is Murrell my father?'

37

AN UNEXPECTED REUNION

They look like us, but scratch their skin
and you'll find corruption and rot.
The Loathsome Witches and All Their Vile Ways
by Dr Mitchel Scanlon

Hecate didn't speak. Instead she lowered her head and began to shake.

'She's crying,' Bramley gasped. 'Does that mean—'

'I feel sick,' Hazel breathed. 'Not him, *please*.'

'Now I come think of it, I can see a resemblance . . .' Bramley mused.

Hecate's skin glowed white with magic that smelt like spring blossom; laughter, not tears, rippled from her like sunlight over water. 'Nicolas?' she gasped. 'Your father? Is that what you thought?'

'You mean he isn't?' Hazel said, overwhelmed with relief.

'Of *course* not. Why would you think that?'

'Well, you know each other from way back, and he seemed really upset that you didn't tell him about me.'

Hecate's laughter faded along with her magic, plunging them back into darkness. 'Nicolas and I are friends . . . *were* friends. But we were never in love. I promise I will tell you everything about my past, the war and your father, if you

220

really want to know . . . but right now we'd better keep going, all right?'

'All right.'

'We should be at ground level now,' Hecate said, taking Hazel's hand and leading her down a passage. 'Ah, here we are. I just hope the mechanism is still working . . .'

A battered wooden bookcase stood against the wall. Hecate grabbed a nearby sconce and gave it a pull. Hazel gave a yelp of surprise as there was a clank and the bookcase swung open on rusty hinges, revealing a low passage behind.

'Secret door,' Hecate said with a grin. 'Follow me.'

They splashed their way down a short, waterlogged passage built into the keep's outer wall. Reflected light rippled on the ceiling. Ten feet or so ahead Hazel saw the end of the passage and the moon-kissed moat beyond. A miraculously dry Hecate and predictably mud-splattered Hazel made their way towards a dilapidated wooden jetty. Water lapped between the boards wherever Hazel stepped.

'Here we go,' Hecate said, climbing aboard an ancient rowboat tethered to a mooring ring. 'This is how I escaped last time, except then you were swelling my belly to the size of a plum duff.'

The boat rocked as Hazel sat on the bow seat, gripping the gunwales to keep her balance. Tom sat in the middle, eyeing the water suspiciously. Hecate shoved the boat away from the jetty and they drifted out into the open.

Using their hands to paddle, they guided the boat across the moat until it nudged the opposite bank. A street of empty houses skirted the moat. The two witches clambered out and scampered into an alley.

'We need to lose ourselves in the forest,' Hazel said. 'Do you know how to get to the main gate?'

'I know every street and yard in Rivenpike,' Hecate replied.

She led Hazel unerringly down alleys, back streets and dank, cobbled yards, muttering street names under her breath with Tom racing at their heels. They jagged left and right, scaling fences and cutting through abandoned houses and workshops.

The route through the ruins seemed random, but Hazel could tell they were heading roughly in one particular direction.

'Not far now,' Hecate said, putting on a burst of speed and disappearing around a corner. Hazel followed, cloak flying – and ran into her mother who had stopped dead in the entrance to a seedy courtyard.

'Why have you—? Oh.'

'Of all the rotten luck,' Bramley wailed.

Titus's wagon stood in the corner. Light glowed from the windows. Hazel put her finger to her lips and both she and Hecate backed towards the alley. 'Ma, there's something I need to tell you,' she whispered. 'I may have . . .'

Paws padded on stone as Samson skittered into the alleyway, causing Tom to jump on to a window ledge and arch his back. Seeing Hazel, Samson bounded over and jumped up, pinning her against a wall with his front paws.

'Gerroff!' she spluttered as the excited dog licked her face. Hecate grabbed his collar and vainly tried to pull him away.

'You!' David emerged from behind the wagon with a blunderbuss clutched in his hands. Hazel thought he had a grim look about him, much changed from the cheerful boy she had met in Watley. He raised the gun and fumbled to pull back the hammer mechanism.

'David,' Hazel called, 'if you fire that thing *they'll* hear. The witch and her spider-demon are not far away.'

The colour leaked from David's face and he banged on the side of the wagon. 'Boss. You'd better come out here.'

A window opened and Titus poked his head out. 'What is it?' he said through a cloud of pipe smoke.

'It's the little witch, Boss. And she's got someone with her.'

Hecate gasped and took a step towards the wagon. 'Titus? Is that really you?'

The Witch Finder squinted at her. 'I must be drunk,' he muttered. '*Hecate?*'

38
OLD ACQUAINTANCES

Demons must be bound by powerful spells;
if they escape, the consequences can be terrible.
Notes on Witchcraft and Demonology *by Dr Neil Fallon*

itus clattered down the wagon steps. 'Put the gun down, boy.'

'Thank my lucky stars,' Hecate said, throwing her arms around him and glowing with pleasure. 'My old friend Titus White.'

'You look the same as you did fifteen years ago,' Titus said.

'So do you.' Hecate reached up and pushed the hair away from his face.

'The old grump's gone bashful,' Bramley said. Hazel leaned heavily against a windowsill, too bewildered to respond.

David hovered uncertainly by the wagon, still clutching the blunderbuss. 'What's going on, Boss?'

Titus ignored him. 'So this little pipsqueak is yours, is she?' he said, looking Hazel up and down. 'Well, well.' Hecate nodded and took Hazel's hand.

'They're Wielders, both of them,' David said, edging

224

closer. 'We've got to arrest them, hand them over to the Witch Hunters.' He grabbed Titus's arm. 'Are you even listening to me?'

'You want to hand a little girl and her mother over to those butchers?' Titus growled.

'They're witches. It's our duty to take them in.'

At last Hazel found her voice. 'David – I thought we were friends.'

David glared at her. 'That was before I found out *what* you are.'

'That's enough.' Titus grabbed the blunderbuss from him. 'We're letting these two go while we nail Murrell.'

'Is that what you're doing here?' Hecate asked. 'Looking for Nicolas?'

'He kidnapped you, tried to kill me and my apprentice, and has been summoning demons. Damn right I'm looking for him.' He turned to Hazel. 'He's still here, isn't he?'

'In the castle, and he's on his own – for the moment. Although Lilith, the witch who attacked David, and her spider-demon are in the town somewhere . . .'

Titus grunted. 'Then we'd better be quick. Tell me everything I need to know.'

As quickly as she could, Hazel told an increasingly astounded Titus about the magic circle, the ceremony, Murrell's pact with Baal and the woodsman's transformation into a mindless soldier under Murrell's command.

'The rest of the Chosen, as Murrell calls them, are

outside the walls rounding up more people to feed to Baal,' she finished.

Titus appraised Hazel with grudging respect. 'Well, slop-sprite, you have been busy.'

'We shouldn't trust a word she says—' David blustered.

'I said, enough,' Titus said.

'We should go,' Hazel said, looking around nervously. 'I want to get out of here before the rest of them come back.'

'Yes,' Titus said. 'We'll find you later. Samson has your scent. Now go.'

Hecate squeezed Titus's hand as she passed. 'It's so good to see you again, Titus.'

The old Witch Finder mumbled something in return as Hazel led Hecate up the alley, with Bramley bouncing up and down on her shoulder and Tom scampering at her heels. They peered on to Tower Road and saw the gatehouse not far away.

'It's getting light,' Bramley said. 'No time to waste.'

'Ready, Ma?'

'Ready.'

A scream ripped through the morning silence.

'That sounded like David,' Hazel said, her heart hammering.

There was a deafening bang followed by an orange flash lighting up the walls, and then a bestial roar of rage.

'Titus,' Hecate cried and she ran back down the alley.

'Ma!' Hazel leaped after her and managed to grab the hem of her robe. 'What are you doing?'

226

'I won't run away leaving them in danger,' Hecate said. 'Not this time.'

'It was their choice to stay,' Hazel said. 'They knew what they were up against.'

There was another scream, louder this time.

'All right,' Hazel said, staring into her mother's determined eyes. 'We'll help them. But . . . you need to wait here for me.'

'Hazel, don't be ridiculous, I'm coming with—'

Hazel pushed Hecate into a doorway. 'Please, Ma, for me. Just wait here. Keep Tom safe.'

'What are you going to do?' Hecate asked, looking at Hazel as if she'd never clearly seen her before.

'I'm a Fire Witch,' Hazel replied. 'So I'm going to start a fire.'

39
FIERY DEATH

After the Witch War, fortune-tellers,
alchemists, astrologers and wise-women all fell
under the suspicious gaze of the Witch Hunters.
England – After the Witch War by Dr Breege Whiten

Hazel sped down the alley, letting her magic flow to the surface. Fire trailed behind her like a cloak; sparks crackled through her hair.

'Be careful,' Bramley said, clinging to her ear. 'Your magic is lethal – I don't want to be a murderer's familiar.'

'Ma was right, we have to help them,' Hazel said.

'Just think of the consequences before you act . . .' Bramley persisted. 'Because one wrong decision can mean a lifetime of guilt.'

The wagon blocked Hazel's view of the courtyard, but as she got closer she sensed frantic activity behind it; flitting shadows, a stirring in the air, the scraping of boots on stone. Emboldened by the magic swirling through her, she skirted the wagon and entered the courtyard. What she saw froze her to the spot.

David and Spindle were locked together like dancers performing a ghastly waltz. Gripping Spindle's front legs, David leaned away from her gnashing fangs until he screamed and slipped on to his back. Spindle bore down on him, gibbering triumphantly.

Titus was sprawled in the gutter like a toppled statue. Lilith, her face framed with an icy mane of hair, straddled his chest with her hands frozen blue around his throat. The smoking blunderbuss lay on the ground, just out of his reach.

In the corner of the yard lay Samson, curled up, unmoving, with two puncture wounds on his neck. Froth bubbled around his mouth. Hazel gave a cry of anguish.

Spindle saw her first. With a hiss, the spider-demon squirted a jet of white silk from its abdomen. Hazel threw her arm up to protect her face and the thread wrapped like a whip around her wrist, sticking fast to the skin. It pulled tight, nearly jerking Hazel off her feet. Without even thinking, she let out a pulse of burning magic.

Fire bit into the thread, sparking and speeding up its length like a lit fuse towards Spindle. The demon howled and juddered away, but the thread was still attached to its spinnerets. Freed, David crawled towards Samson.

'Spindle!' Lilith cried.

Titus bucked, knocking Lilith to the ground. He reached out and curled his fingers around the blunderbuss.

The last few feet of thread were devoured and Spindle was engulfed in a ball of flame, thrashing around the courtyard trailing smoke and jets of steam. Titus cut short Lilith's howl by smashing the blunderbuss into the side of her head. David crawled under the wagon with Samson in his arms as Spindle skittered headlong into the corner and exploded, showering the yard – and Hazel – with warm slime.

'Oh, this is *disgusting*,' Bramley spluttered. 'This smell will never come out of my fur.'

Hazel stood, transfixed with horror at what she had done. She wiped her face and tottered over to Titus, who sat in the gutter rubbing his throat.

'Hello again,' he growled. 'Did you forget something?'

'I thought you might need some help,' she croaked. 'Are you all right?'

'Better than her,' he said, gesturing to Lilith who lay face down next to him. 'Help an old man up, would you?'

David emerged from under the wagon, his face blank with shock. Samson dangled limply in his arms.

'Did Spindle bite him?' Hazel asked.

'She crept up on us,' Titus replied, gently taking the dog from David. 'We didn't even notice until it was too late. Where's your mother?'

'I'm here.' Hecate appeared from the alley. 'Hazel, are you all right?'

'Can you help my dog?' Titus said, his voice cracking. 'He's been poisoned.'

'Let me look at him.' Hecate hurried towards them.

'Take him into the wagon. We need to get moving,' Titus said.

'What about her?' Hazel said.

Titus grimaced, and rolled Lilith over with his boot. 'We

can't take her with us, she's too dangerous. David?'

David stared white-faced at something far away.

'David!' Titus snapped his fingers. 'Hide this witch in one of these houses and tie her up.'

'We should kill her,' David whispered. 'Let me do it.'

'We are *not* murderers,' Titus said. 'We'll come back for her later when we're better prepared. Go on now. Here's some rope.'

David did as he was told while Titus and Hecate carried Samson into the wagon. Hazel climbed into the driver's bench to wait, all the while listening out for the return of the Chosen.

Bramley stroked his tail against her neck. 'Little witch?'

'I'm all right,' she said shakily. Her hands still flickered with magic. Taking a deep breath, she watched the light fade. The little dormouse appeared from her hair and surveyed the courtyard. Spindle's remains smouldered in the corner. A bristling leg dangled obscenely from a windowsill.

Titus climbed out of the wagon hatch and sat next to Hazel, closing the doors behind him. His movements were stiff. Bruises covered his neck and he sounded even gruffer than normal.

'Your mother's seeing to Samson. She says he'll survive.'

'Maybe she could help David by getting the rest of Spindle's poison out of him, too?' Hazel said, handing him the reins. 'It's the poison that's making him hate me, I'm sure of it – it's sort of curdled in him, like milk.'

Titus jerked the reins and the horses clopped down the

231

alley towards Tower Road. The echo of their hoofs and the creak of the wagon seemed terribly loud.

'It's not the poison,' Titus said. 'He hates you because you're a witch.'

A weight dropped into Hazel's stomach. 'But I can't help what I am. I've not done anything wrong. All I've ever done is try to help him.'

'David hates your kind because he's been taught to, in every school lesson, every god-damned church sermon, every news pamphlet, since he was a boy . . .'

'But *you* didn't teach him to hate witches?' Hazel asked.

'No, I didn't.'

'So you . . . you *like* witches?'

Titus glanced at her sidelong. 'Only the ones who don't cause trouble.'

Hazel managed a smile. 'Since when do I cause trouble?'

Titus grunted and turned the wagon on to Tower Road. 'I saw the hatred in him from the start, but I was too drunk to care, let alone do anything about it. I failed him. I've been a poor master.'

'It's not too late,' Hazel said, remembering the warm feeling she'd had when she first saw David smile. 'I'd like for us to be friends again.'

'I think recent events involving witches and their familiars might well have made that impossible.'

They sat in thoughtful silence for a while.

'Look, the gatehouse is ahead,' Titus muttered. 'I hope that godforsaken bridge holds.'

Hazel sat forward, trying to quell the hope rising in her heart. *We're not free yet*, she told herself. *Not by a long shot.*

'Tell me about Murrell,' she said. 'How do you know him?'

'He used to be one of King Charles's most trusted chief ministers, back in the days when witchcraft was tolerated.'

'Before the Witch War.'

'Indeed. He was fascinated by magic and he coveted the power it promised, but he was not a Wielder. So he spent years studying witchcraft until he was the foremost scholar on the subject. But even those closest to him did not know that he was dabbling in the dark art of demonology.'

'Which he did hoping he would be able to gain magical powers?'

'Yes, I think so.'

'So did Murrell—?'

'Quiet now – the bridge is coming up. I'll tell you more when we're safely out of here.'

The creaking of the wagon got louder as they passed into the gatehouse. Across the dilapidated bridge lay the forest, its roof capped green by the early morning sun.

There was a scuffle somewhere behind the wagon. The horses tossed their heads and whinnied. Hazel looked round and saw robed figures emerge from the shops and run towards them. A few had animals by their sides – a dog, a floppy-eared hare, a raven.

So they're Wielders too, Hazel thought.

'It's an ambush,' Titus said. 'They must have heard the

cannon and come back. Damn it to hell!'

Something reared up by the side of the wagon. Hazel caught a glimpse of a horrible face and then the old Witch Finder was gone, dragged from his seat.

The woodsman! Hazel thought, fighting down a wave of panic. *And we were so close to escaping . . .*

She tried to grab the reins but strong hands dragged her off the wagon. She landed heavily on the ground, winded and shaken but still conscious enough to lash out. The blow connected with something soft and there was a gratifying grunt of pain.

But her fightback was cut short. Someone pinned her arms to her sides and then the world went black as a bag made of rough material was dragged over her head. She sensed people pressing in around her, then a voice grated by her ear.

'Try any magic, try to escape, make a noise, and you're all going over the ravine.'

Hazel froze. She heard whispering, then the voice in her ear again. 'We're taking you back to Nicolas. He'll decide what to do with you.'

40
BLIND AND LOST

'Trust no one.'
The Woodsman

F ingers gripped Hazel's arms and a vicious prod in the
back forced her to walk. Her fearful breathing made the
heat inside the bag unbearable. She stumbled a few times,
but the iron grip on her arm never loosened or let her fall.

The ground's sloping up, she thought. *We're going back
to the castle.*

Bramley crawled restlessly around the nape of her neck.
'I can't breathe! You're taking up all the air.'

'That's the least of our problems,' Hazel whispered.

'I don't think Murrell will harm you,' squeaked the little
mouse, pressing his cheek against her skin. 'At least I hope
not. You and your mother are too important.'

Hazel let the idea sink in. 'But what about Titus and
David?'

'I think it's fair to say that they are in deep manure.'

'And what if they find Lilith? Or she gets loose from her
bonds? Murrell won't take kindly to what we did to her, or
her demon.'

235

Bramley didn't respond so they stumbled on in silence, listening to the footfalls and whispers of the witches. Behind her came the woodsman's heavy step; to her left, David's uncertain stumbling, and all around, carried on the breeze, was the tang of blood that she had grown to hate.

A change in the air told her they had entered the market square. Pinpricks of light filtered through the bag.

'That's far enough,' a voice said.

A shove forced her on to the low wall of the fountain. She sensed two others on either side of her. One of them grabbed her hand: Hecate. The other smelt of old tobacco: Titus.

'Get this filthy bag off my head,' he said. 'And where's my dog? If you so much as—'

Someone must have hit him, because he grunted and collided with Hazel's shoulder. Over the sound of her panicked breathing, Hazel heard the witches talking nervously to each other.

'Bram, stay out of sight,' Hazel whispered. 'I don't want them to take you away.' He gave a frightened squeak and burrowed deeper into her hair.

Eventually the whispers stopped and the bag was whipped from her face. Black-garbed witches and their familiars stood around them in a semi-circle. David crouched on the ground like a beaten dog. Leaning on his stick in front of her, with Rawhead by his side, was Murrell.

'Together again,' he said with a thin smile. 'How *nice*.'

Titus pushed himself upright and spat on Murrell's boot.

Rawhead lowered his head and growled.

'Damned dirty demon,' Titus growled back.

'What a strange little family you make,' Murrell said, flicking the spit away with his walking stick. 'It would be a shame if anything happened to you.'

Hazel glared at him. 'We're not going to help you, so just let us go, will you?'

'But we've only just remade our acquaintance,' Murrell said with mock surprise.

'Hazel told me you went down into the Underworld,' Titus said. 'It seems you're paying the price for your folly.'

'I have demon blight,' Murrell replied. 'My flesh is withering, my blood drying up in my veins. I am dying.'

'I should have killed you myself, all those years ago,' Titus said. 'Then the Witch War would never have started.'

'What does he mean by that?' Bramley whispered.

Hazel was surprised to see Murrell wince at Titus's words before turning his black eyes to Hecate.

'I told you I'd find your daughter,' he said. 'And you know what will happen if you refuse to cure me.'

Hecate gathered Tom into her arms and stood up. 'I'll do as you ask, but only after you let my daughter and the two Witch Finders go.'

'Ma, no!' Hazel cried.

'You know I can't do that. If I let Titus go he'll come back with help.' Murrell shook his head. 'And Hazel will never leave your side, not even if you begged her to.'

'Why don't you just get on with it?' David said, his eyes red with angry tears. 'Kill us and be done.'

'I have no wish to kill you, tempting as the prospect is. Hecate, if you cure me I promise to hold them prisoner for the time being. No harm will come to them – you have my word.'

Titus snorted in disgust.

'Don't do it, Ma,' Hazel hissed. 'He can't be trusted.'

'I have no choice,' Hecate said, walking over to Murrell. 'You'd do the same if you were in my position.'

'Watch them while I'm gone,' Murrell said to his followers. 'And someone find Lilith. I need her.'

Hazel watched as Murrell and Hecate disappeared into the castle with Rawhead behind, sniffing the ground. The sun rose, a golden coin gleaming on a flawless blue cloth. It was going to be a beautiful day.

Half an hour or so later, two figures re-emerged from the castle. Murrell strode towards them, tall and strong, just as he had been when Hazel first saw him; but he wasn't *quite* the same – darkness hid behind his smile, as if he was recalling a painful memory.

Hecate followed, looking pale and shaken. She slumped down on to the fountain wall. Hazel put her arms around her, alarmed at how cold she felt.

'I'm all right, sweet-pea. It was a strain, that's all. I just need a minute.'

Hazel wanted to lash out at the beaming Murrell, but she knew that would do no good. *I need to give us all as*

good a chance of escape as possible, she thought. *But how?*

She composed her features into an expression of humble submission and addressed Murrell. 'I've changed my mind. I've been thinking about everything you've said, about Cromwell . . . and the Witch Hunters. I don't want to live my life in fear. I want to help you.'

'Hazel, what are you doing?' Hecate said, trying to grab her arm.

Murrell leaned on his stick. 'So, our little Fire Witch has had a change of heart, has she?'

Hazel stood up. 'I have. I've seen what it's like for witches in England. I realize that it's my duty to join your fight. Cromwell and his Witch Hunters must be stopped.'

'I knew she'd betray us,' David hissed.

'Shut up, boy,' Titus said.

'So you want to join our war?' Murrell asked. 'You want to be a warrior, marching into battle cloaked in fire?'

'Yes,' Hazel said, drawing herself up. 'That's what I want.'

'I'm afraid I don't believe you.' Murrell sighed. 'You're just saying what you think I want to hear.'

'No, really, I—'

Murrell held up his hand. 'No more lies. I see now what I must do.'

'Nicolas?' Hecate's voice trembled. 'You promised me . . .'

'I know, and I'm sorry to break my word,' Murrell said. 'But you are all against me, and I can't leave anything to chance. There is simply too much at stake.'

'What are you going to do?' David breathed.

Murrell smiled sadly and turned to his followers. 'Take them to the church. It's time Baal tasted some human souls.'

41
DEMON FOOD

*Demons crave human souls. Consuming souls gives them
strength and increases their standing among their own kind.*
Necronomicon, *Vol. II* (author unknown)

T he church doors crashed open and Murrell marched
inside with Rawhead in tow. Hazel struggled between
two witches who held her arms tight. Titus fought and
shouted, and under the din Hecate pleaded for them to set
her daughter free. David seemed to be in shock and didn't
make a sound.

'To your places,' Murrell ordered his followers. 'Begin
the containment chant.' The witches raised their hoods,
fanned out and took up their positions around the circle.

A shove sent Hazel pitching forward over the line of salt.
Titus and David stumbled after her. Hecate, still clutching
Tom, was forced down into a pew.

Titus looked at the ugly marks carved into the stone
floor. 'Nicolas, this is *wrong*, and you know it.'

'Right and wrong. It's all a matter of perspective,'
Murrell said. 'Witch Hunters kill witches every day. That's
wrong. But –' he raised a finger into the air – 'Cromwell
would disagree.'

The witches began their dolorous chant. The shimmering barrier rose up from the salt and everything on the other side became wavy and unreal. Cold gripped Hazel, freezing her magic. Her skin tingled with ice.

'After everything we've been through, it's going to end like this,' Bramley said, shivering in her hair.

'At least let these two go,' Titus said. 'For God's sake, Nicolas, they're *only children*.'

'I take no pleasure in this. I do it because I must.'

Titus was red-faced with fury. 'Whatever happens, I'm coming back to get you,' he said. 'And believe me, I will be an especially vengeful ghost.'

Hazel put her hand against the barrier and felt it hum under her fingers. The incessant chant drummed into her brain.

Murrell loomed over her, his eyes burning with intent. 'You will outshine us all, Hazel,' he said. 'A fire warrior with demonic gifts. You will win me my war, but I'm afraid you must say goodbye to your little friend.'

Before she realized his intent, Murrell muttered a spell, reached through the barrier and plucked Bramley from her hair. Hazel threw herself forward, feeling as if her heart had been yanked from its moorings.

'Give him *back*,' she screamed. 'You're *hurting* him.'

'Do you know what happens to a familiar when their witch dies?' Murrell asked, dangling the dormouse by his tail. 'Their heart breaks and they eventually pine away. Such is this little fellow's fate. Don't you think it would be more

242

merciful to give him a quick death?'

Hazel's courage ebbed away, leaving her utterly wretched. She sank to her knees, tears scorching her eyes as she stared at her familiar through the shimmering barrier. 'Please, let us go home. I just want to *go home.*'

Murrell looked down on her, his face softening. 'We've all lost things we loved. It's part of life.' He clicked his fingers. 'Rawhead!'

The demon sat up like a begging dog. Murrell dangled Bramley over its gaping mouth.

Titus knelt and put his arm around Hazel. 'Don't look,' he whispered.

A black hole of panic opened inside Hazel. She tore herself from Titus's grasp and threw herself at the barrier, fire sluicing from her fingers. The barrier bent outward as cracks of shimmering light appeared and began to widen.

The witches chanted louder, reinforcing their magic and closing up the cracks. Hazel's feet slipped. Her magic ebbed, threatening to burn out, but still she forced it to flow until despair gripped her and her flames fluttered and died.

Through her tears she saw the little patch of white under her familiar's chin; the whiskers around his nose; his little, kicking legs.

Murrell opened his fingers. Bramley fell. Rawhead snapped its jaws shut and swallowed.

Hazel sank to her knees, sobbing uncontrollably and unable to even gather the strength to cry out his name.

'It's over,' Murrell said. 'Soon you will have forgotten

all this. Baal will free you of pain, grief and memory. In a few—'

Rawhead choked and a plume of smoke gushed from its mouth. The demon shook its head, looking as surprised as a creature with no eyes could manage.

'What—' Murrell said.

The demon retched so hard all the muscles stood out around its neck, and then a squealing fireball shot out of its mouth, sailed through the air and landed by the door leading to the belfry.

'Bramley!' Hazel cried.

Before Rawhead could give chase, the little dormouse found his feet and disappeared up the spiral staircase – his glow fading as he rounded the first turn. The demon bounded after him, black tongue lashing the air.

'Leave it,' Murrell ordered. 'I want you here.' He rolled up his sleeve to reveal the scars on his arm. 'Brothers, sisters – it is time to call forth our patron.'

Wrapped in a daze, Hazel clambered to her feet and staggered over to Titus and David. The old Witch Finder was looking at the carved marks on the floor, his face pinched with concentration.

'This is not the peaceful retirement I'd hoped for,' he said. 'Who'd have thought it would come to this?'

Murrell's voice cut through the chant, each word ricocheting around the circle like a musket ball. Eldritch light flickered along the lines of the circle and the air filled with the bitter smell of burned almonds. White mist seeped up from the ground, gathering in a swirling ball in the centre of the circle.

Here it comes, Hazel thought, backing away with Titus and David as the mist separated into three tentacles.

'Murrell,' Titus yelled. 'My dog is in the wagon. Do one thing right in your miserable life and look after him, will you?' Without stopping his chant, Murrell nodded.

The tentacles probed closer. Hazel pressed herself against the barrier and closed her eyes. And then a familiar voice cut into her mind.

'*Hazel*,' it whispered. '*Look out. And look up!*'

She sensed a shift in the air directly overhead, as if something huge was moving towards them. Acting on instinct, she threw herself at Titus and David, pushing them towards the edge of the magic circle – just as the ceiling exploded.

She clapped her hands to her ears as the great church bell plummeted from the darkness of the tower in a hail of nails and smashed floorboards. The air vibrated. A trail of orange fire streaked from the top – it was Bramley, clinging on with both paws, eyes tight shut.

Hazel was sure that the world would split in two as the edge of the brass bell struck the magic circle dead centre, sending a fountain of sparks into the air. The floor bucked, knocking Murrell and several witches from their feet and slamming Hazel, Titus and David through the dissolving magical barrier and out of the circle.

The ground split open. Cracks spread, destroying

the magic symbols. The world trembled again as the bell toppled on to its side and rolled in a cacophonous curve.

Bramley, his fur still aflame, leaped from the bell where he'd burned the mounting through, and scampered over to Hazel. With her ears still ringing, she gathered him up to her chest, feeling his heart beat fast against her own.

Someone grabbed her shoulders and pulled her backwards towards the altar. It was Hecate – she was shouting something – but Hazel couldn't hear the words over the howl of the wind rushing up from beneath the cracked church floor.

The smashed stone floor under the bell sagged. Powerful otherworldly magic flashed from somewhere deep below the church, casting a sickly light over everything.

The disintegrating magic circle continued to crack and split – until the bell tumbled into the black pit, tolling dolefully as it fell. The panicked witches and their familiars ignored Murrell's orders and fled for their lives, casting terrified glances at the gaping, jagged hole in the floor, which now stretched across the width of the church.

We're trapped, Hazel thought.

42

THE VOICE OF BAAL

'I don't face death. It faces me.'
Witch Finder Captain Titus White

Hazel and Hecate cowered on the cold stone floor behind the altar. Tom prowled at their feet, hackles raised. The clamour of splitting rocks and fizzing magic died away. The air throbbed, as if pulsing in time to the beat of a malicious heart.

Bramley trembled. 'I'm so sorry, Hazel. This is all my fault.'

'You saved my life, my clever little mouse,' Hazel replied. 'And Titus and David too. You did what you had to do.' Keeping hold of her mother's hand, she peered around the edge of the altar.

The church looked as if it had been struck by a meteor. Pews lay scattered and shattered all over the floor, and a multi-coloured carpet of broken stained glass covered the paving stones.

A crevasse, many feet wide, split the floor like an evil grin. The air over it shimmered and gasped, as if some huge creature was breathing from its depths. Shadows backlit by

247

hellish light swept across the church roof.

The woodsman, the witches and their familiars had gone – fled in terror, or lost into the abyss. Only Murrell remained, crouched on his knees, staring into the darkness with a face masked in shock.

'Look – there's Titus and his boy,' Hecate said. 'They're hiding in the pulpit.'

Bramley appeared behind Hazel's ear and sniffed the air. 'Something's coming,' he said. 'From *down there*.'

He was right. Hazel felt its approach like a sickness. She wanted to back away and hide, but she forced herself to watch as a vast red appendage unfurled from the crevasse. Muscle rippled, moisture dripped; it looked like a giant quivering tongue reaching up to lick the ceiling.

'What is it?' Bramley squeaked.

Murrell gazed up, his face slack with fear.

He knows, Hazel thought. *He's seen it before.*

'Look,' Hecate breathed. 'Something's happening to it.'

There was a wet tearing sound as a split opened at the tip of tongue and ran down both sides. Hazel felt sick as the two halves peeled away, revealing the head and shoulders of a wizened old man. Pallid skin stretched tightly over bones, and only a few strands of hair clung to his scalp.

Hazel thought he must have been long dead, until he opened his mouth and took in a long, rattling breath.

Murrell cowered behind an upturned pew.

The man worked his jaws up and down, left and right, as if he had not used them for years. When he spoke, his voice was dry as bone dust.

'I am he . . . who was once the man called Petrov. I am he . . . who is bound to Baal. I am he . . . who is the Voice of Baal. I speak for Baal to those unworthy of listening.'

Hazel felt Hecate's grip on her hand tighten. Her heart thumped painfully in her chest. *Three days ago I was picking apples*, she thought. *Now I'm face to face with a demon's envoy.*

The appendage swept the once-man Petrov around the edge of the circle. 'Baal demands to know what has happened to his circle,' he said. 'Baal demands to know why his gift has been squandered. Show yourself, the one called Nicolas Murrell. Show yourself to Baal, for Baal knows you are near.'

'Perhaps the demon will take Murrell and leave us alone,' Bramley said.

'Baal would speak with you.' Petrov's voice hardened; there were shards in the bone dust now. 'Come out, Murrell, if you want to keep your skin.'

The pew creaked as Murrell levered himself up. Petrov swivelled towards him. 'Baal sees that the circle gifted to you is shattered. The souls promised to Baal have not been delivered. The bargain struck with Baal has been *dishonoured.*'

Murrell bowed his head. He was shaking and his words came in a whispered rush. 'I prostrate myself before Baal the Destroyer and ask that he forgives his most loyal and humble servant.'

'Baal does not feed on excuses.' Petrov swooped, stopping inches from Murrell's pallid face. 'Baal is hungry for what was promised to him.'

'Please, I know I have failed, but if Baal would give me one more chance . . .'

'Your soul is ruined, Murrell, bitter, worthless and not pleasant to eat. But Baal is hungry *now*. Baal *will feed*.'

'There are others here.' Murrell wept, grovelling on the floor. 'Take them as penance for my failure.'

'The rotten tell-tale,' Bramley hissed.

'There *are* others here – Baal can smell them. But they are not yours to bargain with.' Petrov swept back up into the rafters, sniffing the air and forcing Hazel to duck back. A shiver ran through him. 'Ahh,' he rasped. '*Wielders*.'

43
FLESH-BOUND

'I have communed with the Great Beast.
He will come for me when it pleases him.'
Grand Magus L. G. Petrov

'**H**azel, *whatever* that thing is, it knows we're here,' Bramley said.

'Quiet, Bram, I'm trying to think. Ma, do you think . . .' A stream of blood ran from Hecate's scalp, frighteningly red against her pale skin, and her eyes, usually so bright, were dull and unfocused.

'Ma?' Hazel said, clasping Hecate's face. 'What . . . what happened?'

'I must have hit my head . . . the debris from the ceiling . . .' she said.

'This is all my fault . . .' Bramley wept.

Hazel whipped a handkerchief from her pocket and pressed it against the wound. 'Can you heal yourself?'

Hecate shook her head and mumbled, 'My magic's still weak. Healing Nicolas sapped my strength . . . I can't focus . . .'

'Here,' Hazel said, lifting her mother's hand to the handkerchief. 'Hold this tight.' She looked around for a way out that she'd previously missed, but there was nothing but stone walls, and windows that were too high to reach. 'Don't worry, I'll get us out of this somehow.'

'Wielders,' Petrov continued, his voice now coming from high up in the eaves. 'Two at least, brimming with magic. It would please Baal to talk to them. It would please him also to sate his appetite upon them, should they remain hidden.'

Hazel squeezed her eyes shut. She knew what she had to do, and it seemed that in the end she didn't really have a choice.

'Ma, stay here, and don't make a noise.'

Hecate rested her head against the altar. 'Don't go,' she mumbled.

'I'm going to talk to . . . the thing out there, and get it to let us go. And if I can't, I'll at least put up a fight. And when I do, try to get out while it's distracted.'

Hecate's brow creased. 'You know I'd never leave you, sweet-pea,' she said.

Hazel kissed her brow. 'Just stay here for now.'

'Baal is waiting.' Petrov's voice sounded smoother, as if lubricated by use. 'Come out, come out, wherever you are.'

Hazel picked Bramley up and held him in her palm. 'I can't ask you to come out there with me,' she said. 'Why don't you stay here with Ma?'

'Don't be so ridiculous!' he cried, scurrying up her arm and into her hair. 'I'm not leaving you.'

With shaking legs, Hazel stood up and walked towards the crevasse, doing her best to hide the crippling fear gnawing at her insides. At the same moment, Titus appeared from the pulpit, apparently also deciding to face Petrov.

They nodded to each other and approached the edge of the fissure between their world and the demon's.

Hazel leaned forward and saw a distant glow staining the rock walls red; the bottom, if there even was one, was out of sight. The tongue disappeared into the depths, its length impossible to contemplate.

Petrov swooped down to eye level, close enough for Hazel to see every line in his face and every withered fold of skin. The bands of flesh holding him flexed and pulsed.

'A Fire Witch,' Petrov hissed. 'You burn like the sun – I see it even through my blind eyes.'

Hazel grimaced. 'Yes, I am a Fire Witch,' she breathed. 'But what are you?'

He cocked his head. The wrinkles on his brow smoothed and the tension around his mouth eased. 'I am . . . I am Lars Göran Petrov, from Sweden,' he said in a voice now tinged with an accent. 'I remember a lake. And Viveka and Birgitta—' The muscles around the man tightened and his mouth jerked open in a silent scream.

'What's happening to him?' Hazel cried.

Petrov slumped to one side. The tongue of flesh lifted him back up to the rafters and undulated left and right, as if soothing him to sleep.

A strong hand grabbed Hazel's shoulder and pulled her away from the edge of the crevasse.

'There's nothing you can do for him,' Titus whispered into Hazel's ear. 'He's flesh-bound to Baal.' He shook his head, gazing in wonder. 'Lars Petrov. Can it really be you?'

'You know him?'

'Knew *of* him. Lars was a demonologist who disappeared in the tenth century, in very odd circumstances. It was always rumoured that he tried to consort with demons, and it looks like the rumours were true.'

A shiver ran down Hazel's back. 'You mean he's been like this . . . ?'

'For seven hundred years, yes.'

'Look out – it's coming back,' Bramley said.

'I am he who once was the man called Petrov.' The tongue swooped down to them again. 'Now I am the Voice of Baal. Baal is waiting for that which was promised. Souls to sustain him. Souls to give him strength in the prosecution of his wars.'

'Take his,' Titus said, pointing to the prostate Murrell. 'He is the one who has failed you.'

Petrov curled his lip. 'Baal has tasted that man's soul and found it lacking. But the soul of a Wielder . . . they are most nourishing.'

Hazel's legs threatened to collapse from under her, but she resisted the temptation to grab hold of Titus. Somehow she knew that showing weakness to the demon would be disastrous.

'Baal knows that a soul offered freely is worth more than a hundred taken by force.' Titus stretched his arms out from his sides. 'And I offer him my soul, freely.'

'What are you doing?' Hazel hissed. 'You might become like Petrov.'

Titus ignored her. 'I offer my soul freely on the condition you let the others go.'

Petrov swerved closer to Titus, his lip curling with distaste. 'You are old. Your soul fades like a dying star. Baal will not bargain with you.'

Titus reeled. 'I am a man . . . a Witch Finder . . .'

'Baal knows you, Titus White. He smells your sickness. He says it is time to make your peace.'

Hazel took Titus's hand and directed her fiercest glare at Petrov. 'He's stronger than you'll ever be.'

The ground shook, nearly knocking Hazel from her feet. Cracks appeared in the flagstones. Rock chips and dust cascaded into the crevasse. A great booming, hooting noise welled up from the darkness, battering her ears. She and Titus stumbled backwards. Petrov followed them, smiling.

'What's happening?' Bramley cried.

'Baal is amused by your words, little girl,' Petrov said, as the shaking died away. 'Your bravery puts most men to shame.'

Hazel thrust out her chin. 'If I amuse him so much, let him take me. I offer my soul freely, in return for letting the others go.'

'Don't listen to her, she doesn't know what she's saying,' Titus said, pushing her behind him.

'Yes, I do,' shouted Hazel. 'I'll do it to save Ma – you and David as well.' She reached out her hand to Petrov. 'Baal the Destroyer – *take me*.'

44
SOUL SACRIFICE

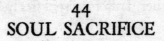

Our healer was arrested by Witch Hunters.
When we are sick, we have no one to look after us.
The Bee and the Honeysuckle by Katherine Agar

A thousand thoughts and a thousand fears charged through Hazel's mind as she said the words, but one shone harshest and most painful of all: *I've condemned Bramley to this fate too.*

Holding an image of her mother walking in the sunlit Glade, she teetered on the edge of the crevasse and whispered, 'Take me, please.'

Petrov edged around her, sniffing, studying, assessing. 'You magic is strong . . . but crude. Baal knows there is another Wielder here. Where is she?'

'I'm here. I am the witch, Hecate Hooper.'

Hazel whirled around and saw her mother emerge from behind the altar, still holding the bloodied handkerchief in her hand.

'Yes,' Petrov hissed. 'Hecate, the Wielder of Life. Baal has heard tell of you.'

'Then he knows what use I could be to him,' Hecate replied.

256

A pit of despair opened up in Hazel. 'Ma,' she shrieked, 'don't you *dare*!'

Hecate nodded to Titus, who returned the gesture and took a firm but gentle hold of Hazel.

'Your mother knows best,' he said, as Hecate walked towards Petrov with Tom clutched in her arms. 'This is the only way we get to stay alive.'

'No, no, *no*!' Hazel struggled to free herself, kicking and thrashing, but Titus held on grimly.

'If you will let the others go unharmed and seal this rift forever, I will go with you willingly,' Hecate said.

Petrov's smile nearly split his face in two.

'Baal . . . agrees.'

The flesh around him loosened and slipped down, releasing his skinny arms. He held them out towards Hecate. 'Baal gives his word, but you must come now. Other events demand his attention.'

Hecate turned to Hazel, her face calm, her eyes bright. 'I'm sorry, dearest daughter. But try to understand why I'm doing this.'

With a hungry leer Petrov swooped down, gathered her and Tom up in his arms, and lifted her from the ground.

With a scream, Hazel sent out a burst of fire, forcing Titus to let her go. The world blurred as she dashed after her mother, trailing sparks and tears. Knowing it was already too late, Hazel jumped over the edge.

Already far below, the tongue coiled back into the Underworld, carrying her mother away.

The breath caught in Hazel's throat as her cloak drew tight around her neck. She hit the rock face with a bone-shaking thud, her arms flailing, then felt herself being dragged back into the church and away from the edge.

'Let me go!' she screamed. 'I want to go with her.'

In her fury she didn't feel the floor shake as the crevasse closed up, or hear Titus trying to calm her down. All she saw was her mother disappearing into blackness, before she did the same.

A fog engulfed Hazel's mind.

The cold stone floor pressed against her back, Bramley warmed the nape of her neck. She was dimly aware of strong arms gathering her up, rough material against her cheek, bumpy movement, glass crunching underfoot, and words spoken in a baritone rumble. Then a rattle, a blinding light and a breeze.

She opened her eyes and saw she was outside under a perfect blue sky. But how could the world still turn unhindered when it had been knocked so far off its axis?

Her mother. *Gone.*

A voice came to her as if through a wall. She forced her eyes open. Titus, looking down at her, brow furrowed. Blood pumped, magic gathered. She shook her head clear and the world encroached again.

'Can you walk?' he was saying. 'Hazel, come back to me.'

Come back to me.

'I'm all right.' Her voice sounded far away. 'You can put me down now.'

Her legs wobbled, but Titus stayed by her side, his shadow cast long in the morning sun. Tombs and crypts came into focus. Ahead, at the entrance to the Garden of the Dead, was David, pushing a hunched, bound and blindfolded Murrell ahead of him.

'I've arrested him,' Titus said. 'But we need to leave quickly before his people regroup.'

Hazel stopped, aware of a presence behind them. Before she even turned around, the smell told her what it was.

Rawhead padded towards them between the rows of gravestone, sniffing the air like a hunting dog. Hazel had only ever seen it shadowed in dusk and darkness, and she was unprepared for the full horror revealed in the morning light. The demon was sleek and lethal, and it had their scent.

Titus and Hazel backed away, the distance between them and the demon less than twenty paces.

'You go on,' Titus muttered. 'Follow David. I'll take care of this.'

'You've got no weapons,' Hazel whispered back. 'It'll kill you.'

'Just go, will you?'

Hazel took a step back and slipped, almost losing her footing. A rotten, fishy smell overpowered Rawhead's blood-stink. It was the remains of the Shabriri demon. The Grinder glinted at her from where she'd left it behind a gravestone – a thousand years ago.

An idea broke through the haze and she grabbed Titus's arm. 'Keep backing up,' she said, gathering the final embers of her magic into a ball around her hand. She raised her arms, waiting for the right moment.

Rawhead stopped closer, jaw lowering like a drawbridge.

'I really think we should run,' Bramley said.

'Your master's over there,' Hazel cried, standing her ground. Rage and a need for vengeance built inside her. 'But you'll have to go through me first.'

Rawhead's back legs quivered, tongue slipped between its teeth.

'I hope you know what you're doing,' Titus growled.

The demon leaped, and as it bounded towards her, Hazel flung her fire at the ground, igniting the fish oil with a *whoosh*. Green flames leaped eight feet into the air, spreading across the paving slabs and filling the air with greasy smoke. Titus grabbed Hazel and pulled her away.

Moving too quickly to stop, Rawhead ran straight into the inferno. The demon slipped and fell forward, legs splaying out beneath it. There was a hiss like roasting meat, and then the flames baking its flesh blossomed red and exploded.

Titus dragged her away, choking on the fumes as the fire died as quickly as it began, leaving behind a dark stain on the ground.

Hazel woke to the creak and roll of the wagon. She was lying on the bed with the hearth warming her toes. Bramley lay by her head on the pillow. It was night-time; she must

260

have slept for hours. Memories filled her mind and she struggled up on to her elbows.

Bramley stirred and yawned. 'Up at last,' he said.

'I've got to go back to the church,' she said. 'Find a way to follow Ma . . . to bring her back.'

'There's no way to the Underworld from there any more.' Titus sat with his feet on the table, looking keenly at her from under his brow. 'It's been sealed off, and a good thing too.'

Hazel swung her legs over the bed, pleased to see Samson fast asleep in front of the fire, the only sign of his wounds being two scars by his neck. 'I'm going to find a way somehow . . .'

'I thought you'd say that,' Titus said, kicking her boots over to her.

'Where's David?'

'Who do you think's driving?'

'And Murrell?' Just saying his name made her heart ache with fury.

'Tied to the roof.' Titus picked up his pipe and cleaned the bowl out with his thumb. 'The boy was all for taking you both to London. For the bounty, you understand.'

'But you disagreed.'

'I don't work for Cromwell. Besides, you may be foolish and stubborn, but you're not a criminal.'

'Murrell is.'

'Indeed. And believe me, I could retire comfortably on the money on his head. But he's also the only man alive who

261

has ever been to the demon world and survived. Which means . . .'

Hazel's eyes widened. 'Which means if we want to find Ma, we need his help to do it.'

Titus jabbed his pipe at her. 'Exactly.'

It took the rest of the day and the following night for them to reach Mary's cabin, during which time they stopped only once to rest the horses. Hazel had just fallen into a doze, with Samson lying on her feet and Bramley nesting in her hair, when the door opened and Titus looked in.

'We're here,' he said.

Shaking off her weariness, she stepped outside, blinking in the warm summer sunlight. The wagon was parked behind Mary's cabin by the vegetable garden. Grey clouds lay heaped on the horizon like great piles of ash, but overhead the sky was clear and the sun had already warmed the grass under her feet. Hazel was relieved to see that the grave she'd dug for Mary was undisturbed.

I hope she found the peace she wanted, she thought.

David led Hercules over to Titus, his face impassive under the black scarf tied around his eye. Titus handed him a few coins. 'We'll need some food and supplies. We may be here some time. Take the dog with you.'

David climbed on to Hercules's back.

'I know this is not working out how you wanted, David,' Titus said. 'But it's the right thing to do.'

'You're the boss, Boss.'

David avoided even so much as looking at Hazel. He jabbed his heels into Hercules's flank and trotted away with Samson by his side. Hazel and Titus watched him disappear into the trees.

'No reward,' the old Witch Finder said. 'A glorious entry into London with Murrell and a Fire Witch in chains. Just a disfigured face and a life-lesson hard learned.' He shook his head. 'I think I may be losing him.'

'What have you done with Murrell?' Hazel asked. Bramley shuddered behind her ear.

'I've tied him up in the outhouse for now. I'll let him stew for a bit. You get on inside and light the fire. You can do that, can't you?'

'I think so.' Hazel managed a small smile.

'Find them, bind them, burn them.'
Witch Hunter Captain John Stearne

Hazel lay in Mary's bed with a heavy head and a heavier heart. She sat up, blinking as the first rays of the sun crept through the window and the hole in the roof. Bramley stirred in her pocket and poked his head out, blinking sleepily.

'Have you slept at all?' he said, giving himself a wake-up shake.

'Not really.' Hazel rubbed her eyes. 'I feel all foggy and confused. I don't know what to do. How are we going to get Murrell to tell us what we need to know?'

'We've been indoors for too long, and thinking too much. Why don't we go out for some fresh air? Maybe find an apple tree to plunder?'

The thought of a cool breeze and a wash in the stream was appealing. 'All right, why not?' Hazel picked the little dormouse up and tiptoed downstairs to the kitchen. She was a little surprised that the old Witch Finder was not still dozing in the rocking chair where she'd left him last night.

'I wonder where Titus is,' she said.

'Perhaps he's seeing to the horses.'

The forest was eerily quiet, although the sound of the chattering stream lifted Hazel's spirits. Verdant patches of clover, their purple blooms waving in the breeze, grew in the trees' shadow not far from the cabin. Hazel walked through them, enjoying the feeling of wet leaves against her legs.

'It's nice to be outside again,' Bramley said. 'I've missed the feeling of the sun on my whiskers.'

Hazel froze as she bent down to pick some blooms. *There's someone behind me!*

Before she could move, a hand clamped over her mouth and dragged her into the undergrowth skirting the trunk of an oak tree. Fighting panic, she twisted around to see her assailant. Her eyes widened. It was Titus.

He put a finger to his lips. Hazel nodded and he released her. 'Whatever happens,' he whispered, 'don't make a sound.'

Hazel's scalp crawled at the sound of slow footsteps crunching across the vegetable garden and heading towards the cabin. Hardly daring to breathe, she peered cautiously around the tree.

Creeping along a nearby row of cabbages was a helmeted soldier wearing a tarnished breastplate over a dark red tunic, with white facings on the cuffs. He had a sword on his hip and carried a wheel-lock musket in both hands; as he passed the tree he blew on the glowing slow-match.

265

'Roundheads,' Titus whispered. 'Cromwell's men.' He pointed across the vegetable garden. More soldiers emerged from the forest, crouched low and converging on the cabin. 'A company, at least.'

They'll find Murrell, Hazel thought in a panic. *And without him I'll never be able to get into the Underworld.* Without thinking, she lunged forward.

Titus grabbed her waist and pulled her back behind the tree, clamping his hand over her mouth again. 'Don't be stupid,' he hissed. 'There's nothing we can do, there're too many of them. Count yourself fortunate that you're not being collared as well. Just as well I hid the wagon in the forest, or they'd be all over that too. Now *keep still*.' He leaned forward. 'Wait a minute – who's this?'

Hazel stopped struggling as a man in black trousers, shirt and muddy boots stalked out of the trees by the cabin, resting a heavy wooden club over his shoulder. Despite wearing no armour, it was clear by the way the soldiers regarded him that he was in charge. She shivered at the brutal strength packed into his limbs, and the way he walked – like a dog used to winning its fights.

'Captain John Stearne. The Witch Butcher himself,' Titus muttered. 'Of all the scoundrels . . .'

'We can't let them take Murrell,' Hazel begged.

'We must,' Titus said.

Stearne stopped by the cabin, close enough for Hazel to see his flattened nose and dark eyes. He nodded to the Roundheads, who knelt in front of the cabin and trained their muskets on the windows. Four more stood with their backs to the wall next to the cabin door, and two others readied themselves by the outhouse.

They waited, eyes on Stearne. At his signal the soldiers kicked the cabin and outhouse doors open and then plunged inside.

'How did they find us?' Titus muttered. 'Why are they even looking?'

Hazel watched as the soldiers dragged Murrell from the outhouse. Stearne strolled up to him and threw a mallet-like fist into his stomach. The demonologist dropped to the ground, doubled up, fighting to breathe.

A soldier poked his head out of the upstairs windows. 'Place is empty, sir,' he called down.

'No sign of the girl or the drunkard?'

'No, sir.'

'Drunkard indeed . . .' Titus grumbled as he pulled Hazel deeper into the thicket.

Stearne turned to one of his men. 'Get the cage, and you might as well bring the songbird round as well. I've got some more questions for him about this merry little band.' The soldier nodded and jogged up the track into the forest.

Stearne surveyed his men as they searched the cabin and garden, clattering up and down the stairs and trampling over the vegetable patches. For the whole time he kept his foot on Murrell and thumped the gnarled end of his club into the palm of his hand.

There was a rumble from the forest track as an enclosed

cart hauled by two horses approached the cabin. It was built from heavy timber and had only one barred window. The crossed-hammer symbol of the Order of Witch Hunters was emblazoned on the side.

Titus's beard scraped Hazel's cheek as he leaned over her shoulder. 'No,' he said. 'It can't be.'

Following his gaze, she saw a shaggy dog trotting down the road behind the wagon. Her eyes widened. 'Is that . . . ?'

'It's Samson,' Titus said.

'If they've got Samson,' Hazel said, 'they must have . . .'

Samson stopped and turned back towards the forest, ears pricked. His tail wagged as David rode out of the trees' shadow, into the dappled sunlight. Two cavalrymen rode on either side of him with matchlocks over their shoulders.

'They've got him prisoner,' Bramley squeaked.

'Wait a minute,' Hazel said. The sun glinted on something at David's hip. It was his pistol. 'He's still armed.'

Hazel and Titus stared as David reached the cabin, dismounted and shook Stearne's hand.

'Well done, lad,' Stearne said. 'You've helped us catch the most wanted man in England, and that will certainly please the General. As for the other two – well, I'm sure we'll find them soon enough.'

When the crashing, shouting and bellowing finally stopped, Hazel cautiously opened the door to Mary's cabin and peered inside. Her eyes were red but she had wiped away the last of her tears.

No more crying, she had told herself, while she listened to Titus venting his fury on the contents of the cottage. *Not any more.*

Stearne and his men had left hours ago, taking Murrell and the vital knowledge he possessed with them. Now, Titus stood alone, chest heaving, in the middle of the kitchen. Broken dish fragments and the splintered remnants of the rocking chair lay scattered around him. The heavy oak table rested on its side against the fireplace.

'Have you finished?' she asked.

Titus turned his stormy glare on to her, fists bunched. 'He betrayed me. The little turd *betrayed* me!'

'I know,' Hazel said. 'Perhaps we should have seen it coming.'

'The bond of loyalty between Witch Finder and apprentice is unbreakable.' Titus shook his head as if trying to recover from a punch.

'Evidently not,' Bramley said.

'He even took my dog, damn his eyes,' Titus grunted.

Hazel picked up a fallen chair and sat down. 'What will happen to Murrell?' Her voice sounded far off, as if spoken by someone else.

Titus slumped into a corner and rested his head against the wall. 'They'll take him to London to face the Witch Hunter General. He'll be interrogated, then they'll probably make a big show of his execution.'

'I need to talk to him before that happens,' Hazel said. 'If I don't, my mum stays trapped with that demon forever.'

269

'London is crawling with Witch Hunters and inform-ants – you won't last five minutes,' Titus said with a wave of his hand. 'And how are you going to get to him? He'll be kept in Hunter's Tower, the most secure gaol in England. And even if by some miracle you do get to speak to him, what makes you think he's going to help you?'

'I'm going.'

He looked at her with sad eyes. 'Nothing I can say will change your mind, will it?'

Hazel held his gaze. 'No.'

'Then we'll go together. After all, I've got my own score to settle.' He clambered to his feet and looked down at her. 'An old Witch Finder and a foolish witch,' he said. 'A strange pair aren't we, slop-sprite?'

'You can come on one condition,' she replied, managing a small smile. 'You have to call me Hazel.'

EPILOGUE

London, July 1655

Witch Hunter General Matthew Hopkins, the most feared man in England, beckoned the boy into his office with a smile. 'You have a message for me?' His voice was like unsheathed steel – smooth and cold.

The boy, about fourteen and wearing the scarlet uniform of a Witch Hunter's apprentice, couldn't stop a shiver running down his back. 'Yes, sir,' he said. 'It's from Captain Stearne. His rider arrived this morning.'

Hopkins gazed at the boy, letting the seconds drag in order to feed on his discomfort. 'Proceed,' he said, when he had tasted enough. The boy cleared his throat.

'General,' he read. 'A stroke of fortune during my purge of the West. I've plucked a juicy apple for you to hang from the Witch Tree. You've taken a bite from it before – perhaps this time you'll cut off more than just his thumb. I'll be back in London soon. Captain John Stearne.'

'Nicolas Murrell,' Hopkins said with a smile on his

liver-coloured lips. 'At last – a worthy candidate to put in the Dark Room.'

He reached out a pudgy hand to a fruit bowl. The apples had been in there for weeks and were nicely brown and puckered. He chose one with a thick rind of mould and plucked it out.

Keeping his ice-pale eyes trained on the messenger, Hopkins took a deep bite from the apple and chewed slowly. The boy's attempt to hide his disgust was a gratifying failure.

Through a mouthful of rotten pulp, Hopkins said, 'Don't hover by the door, lad. *Come in*. Now, read it to me again. I want to savour every word.'

ABOUT THE AUTHOR

Matt Ralphs was born in North Lincolnshire and grew up in Kent. So, by way of a median average, he's from Cambridge. After completing his English Literature degree he was absolutely certain that he didn't know what to do with his life. He eventually drifted into an editorial career in publishing.

After years of having the temerity to tell professional authors what they were doing wrong, he decided to put his limited knowledge to use and pen his own book. *This* book.

Matt lives and floats on a canal boat in London. *Fire Girl* is his debut novel.

ACKNOWLEDGEMENTS

Writing a novel is a task for one person. Turning it into a book takes a team.

Firstly I'd like to thank all the volunteers behind the brilliant Undiscovered Voices competition, and especially Catherine Coe, who suggested I enter. Being chosen as a finalist gave me a huge confidence boost and led directly to me finding a literary agent.

And that agent is tireless champion Madeleine Milburn. Thank you, Maddy, for everything you've done for me.

A big wave and a grateful grin to everyone at Macmillan Children's Books! Rachel Kellehar, my patient and owlishly wise editor; Catherine Alport, promotions extraordinaire; Kat McKenna, mistress of marketing; and the design team who have made the book look *so* damn smart.

I owe a debt to my great friend Breege, whose sage advice still rings in my ears as I write.

And to my family, who supported me in all my wishful endeavours and who, most importantly, brought me endless cups of tea as I frowned and rewrote, frowned and rewrote.

Finally to all the authors – far too many to mention here – who inspired in me a love of words and stories: my eternal thanks to each and every one.

Find out what happens to
Hazel and Bramley
in the searing sequel

FIRE
WITCH

Coming soon!